EL

I

SKER

By the same author

PORTHCAWL—its History and Development

LEGENDS OF PORTHCAWL AND THE GLAMORGAN COAST

THE BREAKWATER

INN OF FEAR

ELIZABETH

Fair Maid of SKER

BY

ALUN MORGAN

PORTHCAWL

COMPUTER @ BOOKSHOP

1997

Reprinted 1997

ISBN 0 953005 00 3

Printed in Wales by

D. Brown and Sons Limited
Cowbridge and Bridgend
Glamorgan

PREFACE

STORIES OF BEAUTIFUL, high-born maidens falling in love with common men has been a theme often repeated in Welsh folk-lore. Perhaps the best known is the romance between the Maid of Cefn Ydfa and Wil Hopcyn at Llangynwyd. But when the analytical eye of historians has been cast on these versions they have often been found false, or at best over-garnished by time and sentiment.

The story of the Maid of Sker, however, seems to be substantiated by a great deal of factual evidence. Elizabeth Williams did live at Sker; she was married to a Mr. Kirkhouse at Llangyfelach church in September 1766; she was loved by Thomas Evans the harpist of Newton (otherwise why the song?); and she was buried at Llansamlet in January 1776, having died just before reaching her thirtieth birthday. Furthermore, it is a fact that her father, Isaac Williams, became greatly disliked in the neighbourhood because of his clandestine activities over the filching of cargo from the wreck of a French vessel, *Le Vainqueur*—thus robbing the local population of its "fair share" of expected loot.

Having lived within walking distance of Sker House for over fifty years, I have been constantly fascinated by this story. I have delved into it from many angles, dissected it, and thrown the pieces into the air; and always they have come down to form more or less the same picture. Whether reading Mr. Leslie Evans' erudite "Sker House", poring over church records, consulting old books, or even getting the regulars of the *Plough and Harrow* at Llansamlet to search for the Maid's missing gravestone, I have been impressed by one thing: the story must have been basically true. The only ingredient missing was how it all came about, for historical research does not always reveal the full extent of human foibles such as love, hate, anger and jealousy—all of which played a prominent part in this drama. The difficulty therefore was to choose the best way to present the material I had gathered. I could have written a straight-forward, factual account, but this would have been short and probably dull, and so I decided to emulate some illustrious forebears and tell the story in narrative form, which at least gives me the opportunity to plumb the depths of passion engendered, without which the story loses its meaning. In doing so I have tried to retain all the known facts, using imagination only when common sense and intuition have indicated that a particular course of action was both plausible and likely (as, for example, when the Maid married at Llangyfelach and not at Maudlam, her family church). I believe this to be the best approach for the general reader, who knows the story only vaguely, or who has been confused by R. D. Blackmore's fictitious heroine. Indeed, having assimilated so many facts and weighed so much available information, I can think of no other way to account for the events; and so this is a conscientious attempt to tell the story as I believe it must have happened, which is probably as near the truth as anybody is ever likely to get. To my way of thinking only one mystery now seems to remain: the whereabouts of Elizabeth Kirkhouse's tombstone, which has disappeared without trace. If anyone can throw a light on this I would be pleased to hear from them.

SKER HOUSE AND ITS SURROUNDINGS

It is not difficult to understand why it is that Sker House should have become the centre of several romances and strange legends. Gaunt and eerie, situated entirely on its own near a vast beach and on the edge of a wilderness of heath and sand, it asks for tales to be woven around it. If one walks there at any season of the year, with the continuous roar of the surf a background for the cries of curlews, peewits and seagulls, one sometimes catches a sense of foreboding and loneliness—"a very sad and lonesome place," as R. D. Blackmore described it, "close to a desolate waste of sands and the continual roaring of the sea upon black rocks".

The present house, re-built in Tudor times, creaks and groans in the wind, "a great grey house with many chimneys, many gables and many windows, yet not a neighbour to look out on, not a tree to feed its chimneys". Its vast rooms have often been the last resting place for sailors drowned after a ship has struck the nearby rocks or keeled over on the frightening, shifting sand known as the Scarweathers.

And yet the region has its beauty, with many strange birds and a host of unusual plants finding a home in its constantly moving sand dunes. A peculiar magnetism ensnares visitors, making them return time after time; a magnetism that must have been felt as early as the ninth century when the Vikings appeared and named the place Sker—Scandinavian for scar or reef. Later the monks of Neath Abbey set up a grange there and farmed the surrounding land, and when they disappeared after the dissolution of the monasteries the de Turbervilles (the descendants of the tough Norman knights of the Conquest) took up residence, retaining the old Catholic faith and making the house a meeting place for Roman priests, who hid in the massive walls. After them came a long line of gentleman farmers, one of them being Isaac Williams, the father of the Maid, who was himself connected by marriage to the Turbervilles. He took over the estate on the death of his father in 1741 and quickly became prominent as the Constable of the Hundred of Newcastle. Although the record of the birth of his daughter, Elizabeth, has not been found, it is she who has been generally accepted as the Maid of Sker.

Near Sker House lies Kenfig Pool, a land-locked freshwater lake of approximately eighty acres situated about 1,000 yards from the sea. Legend has it that the ancient "city" of Kenfig lies submerged beneath its surface, but in actual fact the town was built a little way to the north. A series of great storms, beginning about the year 1300, followed by long periods of drifting sand, eventually buried it completely, and all that remains today are the ruins of the Norman keep. The town hall of the later borough (a "rotten" borough which sent two M.P's. to Parliament until the nineteenth century) is today the *Prince of Wales* Inn.

As might be expected with a buried town, a mysterious pool and a house situated entirely on its own on the moors, stories of ghosts abound in the area. Some of them are of the general variety believed in throughout Wales, such as the Gwrach y Rhibyn (Hag of the Mists), a lost soul who went around uttering fearful cries; a white horse which indicated the certainty of death to the beholder; and the Cyhiraeth, a ghostly wailing or shrieking sound, the harbinger of a forthcoming storm or wreck. Special to Sker, however, is the Great Stone. This stone, lying in a field off Water Street, was said to visit Traeth Morfa every Christmas morning before cockcrow, where it would have a drink of sea-water before returning to its resting place. Anyone unfortunate enough to see it suffered a terrible fate. Sker House itself has a secret recess known as the Abbot's Walk where the ghost of a monk is seen, a quarrelsome fellow who fell out with his brethren and came to an untimely end. Finally, of course, there is the ghost of Elizabeth Williams herself, which has been seen in the room where her irate father imprisoned her.

PRELUDE

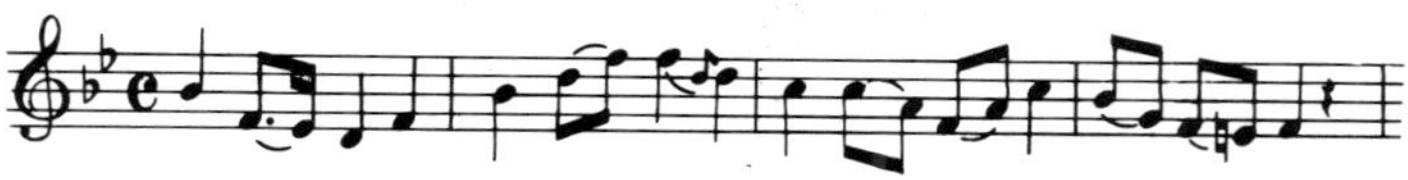

CHAPTER 1

WITHOUT LOWERING her crochet work old Janet Leyson glanced at the fire in the kitchen hearth. From the pile of logs smoke was rising rapidly, sucked upwards by the wind rushing across the chimney pots far above; but occasionally it billowed back, engulfing griddle, turning spit and saucepans in a sooty, black haze. She pursed her lips and concentrated again on the hook. She hated Sker House in a storm, especially in the middle of winter.

All the sounds of a particularly violent gale were present that night: the moaning of draughts around ill-fitting doors and windows; the fluctuating whistle from up near the gables; the constant booming and thudding of waves on the nearby beach; and the long-drawn-out hiss as spray cascaded on the fields around Pwll Dafan. She was familiar with everything but was still afraid, and took little comfort from the fact that the building had withstood similar buffetings for over three hundred years. Always, she reasoned, there was a chance the roof might come off, and she was convinced that the walls, four feet thick though they were, moved slightly under the pressure of the wind; and to make things worse that night a door was banging somewhere outside in the yard. For eighteen years she had been housekeeper to Isaac Williams, the tenant of the manor, but now she wished she had left two months ago when her mistress had died, and gone back to her native Bryncethin where trees and houses afforded shelter. There was no shelter near Sker House. It stood, gaunt and eerie, alone on the moors of Kenfig.

But it was too late for that now. She had promised Catherine Williams that she would look after her two daughters, Mary and Elizabeth, at least until they were of age; and she had never gone back on her word, least of all to her late mistress. Poor Catherine! She could see her gravestone now, cold and wet in nearby Maudlam churchyard, the earth around it still fresh and not settled in. She could even visualise the lettering on the slab, as plain as though it was in front of her:—

Underneath lyeth the body
of Catherine Williams
the wife of Isaac Williams
of Sker who died the 1st day
of October 1753 aged 36

At least the word "beloved" had not been inscribed in front of "wife". Even Isaac Williams had not had the audacity to do that. If anyone had put his wife in her grave it was he, with his philandering and evil temper, and everyone in the parish knew it. Even when his wife was in her last throes he had visited some woman in Nottage, spending the night with her; and already there were rumours of a bastard on the way. Why, Janet wondered, did God sometimes strike down the righteous and spare the unworthy? Perhaps it was because He wanted yet another angel for His host, and Catherine Williams had certainly been an angel whilst on earth. But it was hard for those who were left to have to bear the likes of Isaac Williams.

Still without moving her head she watched the two girls sitting opposite her, one on each side of the table, busily engaged in winding balls of wool. Elizabeth, aged seven, was fair, with vivid blue eyes, almost the image of her mother. Mary, two years older, was darker, taking after her father's colouring. Their natures were different, too. Elizabeth was the generous one, sharing her toys and possessions with anyone; but Mary was harder and more calculating, again like her father. It was difficult for Janet to hide her preference for Elizabeth, but she tried, stifling any indication of favouritism; and she was fortunate that the sisters were usually amicable with each other, with quarrels and tantrums rare. But when they did have differences Janet noticed that

Elizabeth could hold her own: she was not always the placid, yielding creature her mother had been, which was not surprising, knowing that some part of her was Isaac Williams.

Isaac was outside somewhere now, even on a night like this, probably down at Nottage again with his slut. At least he would not marry her: as magistrate and Constable of the Hundred of Newcastle he had a high position in the County, so if he did take a second wife it would be some aristocratic woman, preferably wealthy, for the farm required constant capital. If that happened Janet would have to think again, promise or not, for the new mistress might take a dislike to her, even dismiss her. But that was in the future. Of more importance now was the fact that Isaac's supper was burning in the oven, and had been for two hours. Suddenly Janet's dislike for her master flared; she had spent all the afternoon preparing vegetables, meat and gravy. It was nothing new for Isaac to spoil a good meal by being late, but it had happened too often of late and she was getting tired of it. She stopped crocheting and lowered the hook to her lap.

"Diawch! I don't know where your father can be on such a night."

"Oh!" said Mary in a tone that told Janet she was in one of her condescending moods. "He's out in the cow shed, I expect. One of the cows is sick with the croup. He said that before he went out."

"Did he, now?" rasped Janet. "I don't remember him saying so. Anyway, he was with that dratted cow all this morning. He wouldn't be there now, surely, not as late as this."

"Well, perhaps he's gone down to the beach," said Mary, still cool and unconcerned. "Mark Edwards was saying something about a ship being sighted earlier on. Perhaps they've gone to look for it. Mark said there might even be a wreck and if there is they'll be able to have ten shillings for every drowned sailor they find. They—"

"Taw sôn, Mary!" Janet tried to keep the irritation out of her voice. She disliked Mark Edwards, the foreman, almost as much as Isaac Williams. "If there's a ship out there Mark

Edwards should be praying for the sailors, not thinking what he could get out of it. It's just like him, though. Always on the make. If I catch him around my eggs again I'll box his ears, see if I don't."

"But there could be a wreck, Janet," Mary persisted. "Old Nathaniel from Waun y Mer was telling everybody yesterday that he'd seen the White Horse, and you know what that means, don't you? He also said he'd heard the Cyhiraeth, and that's a sure sign something terrible is going to happen."

Janet retrieved the hook and struck vehemently at the wool, nearly splitting a thread.

"You and your big ears, Mary! Don't listen to such prattle. Nathaniel Evans is a fool, with a tongue too big for his head."

Elizabeth stared at her sister with wide open eyes.

"What's the Cyhiraeth, Mary?"

"A sound, silly, a ghostly sound that people hear just before a ship is wrecked. Everybody knows that. It goes oooooo—!"

"Mary!" Janet's voice was laced with venom. "Stop it this instant. You'll frighten your little sister."

Mary made a face at Elizabeth.

"Frighten her? Nothing ever frightens Elizabeth. If that old stone from Water Street should walk in here now she'd just look at it and say 'How do you do, Mr. Stone? Have you brought me anything for Christmas?' Wouldn't you, Elizabeth? Or if she saw the Hag of the Mists coming towards her on the moors like this—" She held up hands like talons. "Or even if that old monk who lives in the cellar should rattle his chains—"

Janet slammed down the entire crochet work.

"Mary! That's the last time I'll tell you. Any more of that and you'll go straight to bed. For shame on you with your mother not long dead. Elizabeth's only seven. You should act like a mother to her now, not frighten and tease her. Anyway, you do tempt fate talking about things you know nothing about. There are things out on them moors that even grown-ups don't understand, leave alone a child like you."

"I'm not a child any more," said Mary petulantly. "Elizabeth's the child."

"All the more reason for you not to frighten her. I shall speak to your father when he gets back. And anyway, if he don't come soon his supper'll be ruined—burned to a frazzle, and then there'll be a to-do. Oh, well! It's his fault, not mine. He's only got himself to blame."

"Sh!" Mary imperiously raised a fore-finger. "I think there's someone in the porch now. I expect it's father."

They listened and within a few moments the door opened accompanied by a rush of wind. Isaac Williams came in with a storm lantern. He shut the door with difficulty, bolted it and threw his top-coat and tricorn on a chair.

"Uffern! What a night. I swear the stable roof's lifting."

Janet went to the oven and took out the plate of dinner. Unceremoniously she dumped it on the table.

"Don't blame me if your supper's no good by now."

Isaac eyed the plate with little interest and went to the fire. He warmed his big hands, turning them over and over as though he was washing them.

"I'll have it in a minute. I want to warm up first. It's beginning to sleet."

"Where've you been all night?" asked Janet.

"Out," said Isaac evasively. "Out seeing to things. This storm's shaking everything loose. The rick's leaning sideways. I doubt if there'll be a straw left by morning."

Janet sniffed.

"There's been a door banging all night. If there's anything I can't abide it's a door banging in the middle of the night."

Isaac went to the table and desultorily began pecking at his meal with a fork.

"It's the stable door. I'll fix it in the morning. Can't do anything tonight with the wind as it is."

"How's the cow, father?" asked Mary, giving him a bright smile.

Isaac stared at her as though he had not heard correctly.

"The cow? Oh, she's all right. Leastways she should be by tomorrow, that is if the shed roof don't blow away."

"Is there any news of a ship?" asked Janet, who remembered the last wreck at Sker when the kitchen had been full of half-drowned sailors. "Mary here says there's been one sighted."

Isaac's eyes took on a crafty look.

"Who's been telling you that, Mary?"

"Mark Edwards, this afternoon."

"Did he, now? Maybe. I don't know. Mark's always on the look-out for ships. He spends half his time looking out to sea."

"And I know why," said Janet acidly. "Only two years ago there were five dead sailors in that stable of yours and they weren't all drowned either from what I could hear."

Isaac gave her a dark look before spearing a lump of potato.

"Hold your tongue, woman. The children are present. They can hear you. Why haven't you put them to bed?"

"They'll be going presently as soon as they finish that wool. You want your stockings darned, don't you?"

Elizabeth's blue eyes focused unwaveringly on Janet.

"What d'you mean, Janet—the sailors weren't all drowned?"

"She means," said Isaac quickly, "that some of them were killed by being driven against the rocks. Very few men can live once they get on those rocks in a gale."

"Aye," said Janet, realising her mistake. "That's what I meant, merch fach, and I pray for any poor soul out there tonight. You must pray, too, the both of you, before you go to bed."

"Yes, Janet, we will," said the girls together.

Mary came to the end of her ball and looked round for more wool.

"Any more to do, Janet?"

Janet, who had only just picked up her crochet work, set it down again.

"No, no more for tonight. Come on, you two. It's time for bed. Your father do want some peace and quiet down here."

Elizabeth decided to play for time.

"What's the Cyhiraeth, father?"

Isaac stared at her. For a few moments he remained silent, chewing.

"Why d'you want to know about the Cyhiraeth? Who's been telling you about that?"

"Mary," said Elizabeth. "She said Nathaniel Evans heard it yesterday."

"Did she now?" Isaac swallowed and beckoned to both girls. "You're too young to know about things like that. Mary! I don't want to hear any more talk about the Cyhiraeth or any such thing. Do you understand?"

"Yes, father," said Mary contritely.

"That's what I've been telling her," said Janet severely. "I couldn't get her to stop."

Isaac kissed his daughters in his usual desultory, half-hearted manner.

"Then off to bed with the two of you. Sleep well and forget about the storm—and the Cyhiraeth."

Mary leaned up against his chair, still hoping for a remission.

"Yes, father, but if there's a wreck on the beach tomorrow, can we come and look at it?"

"I'll see," said Isaac evasively. "But if you pray as Janet says there'll be no wreck, I'm sure. So off to bed, the two of you. Goodnight."

The girls took the balls of wool to the dresser and dropped them into the work-basket. Elizabeth was about to pick up her doll when there was a loud knocking on the porch door. Isaac nodded to Janet who slid back the bolt and admitted Mark Edwards, streaming with moisture. Isaac pushed his plate aside.

"Well, Mark! What news?"

"It's a vessel all right, sir," said Mark, wringing out a sodden felt cap. "No doubt about it now. She's just clearing the Scarweathers and making for the rocks."

"There!" cried Mary triumphantly. "I told you. Old Nathaniel was right after all."

"Quiet," roared Isaac; then to Edwards: "She'll clear the point, though, won't she?"

"I doubt it," said Edwards. "She'll be aground in twenty minutes, I'd say, or I ain't your gaffer. Half an hour at the most. I don't think anything can save her now, and Willy Llewelyn's of a like mind, too."

Isaac went over to the chair and began pulling on his topcoat.

"What size is she?"

"Fairish as far as I could make out. By the look of the rigging she's foreign. Willy thinks he can see a stack of bales for'ard and she's dragging a mast to starboard. I don't give her a cat in hell's chance with a list like that."

"Then we'd better get down there." Isaac reached for his tricorn and slammed it on his head. "Are all the men ready, like I told you?"

"Aye, sir. Ready and waiting, and as many carts and horses as we could muster. All standing by like you said."

"Anybody else spotted her, d'you think?"

"That I don't know. She might have been sighted off Aberafon, in which case the excise men'll be here soon."

"Then the sooner we get there the better, before half the population of Kenfig turns up. We only want an hour or so."

Isaac began priming the lantern then caught sight of Janet and the children staring at him.

"What are you standing there for? I told you to take the girls to bed, Janet."

Janet glared at him and shepherded her charges towards the hall door. Isaac watched her for a moment.

"And don't wait up for me. If there's a ship on the reef

there'll be rescuing to be done and cargo to be salvaged. It might take all night."

He looked knowingly at Edwards who grinned slyly back. Then both men went out into the storm.

CHAPTER 2

JANET WATCHED the children kneeling in prayer, one on each side of the four-poster bed, and nodded in approval as they asked for God's blessing on all the sailors at sea that night. Then she drew back the heavy side-drapes and deftly removed the two small warming pans. The girls needed no second bidding to clamber into bed for the room, like everywhere else in Sker House away from the fires, was icy cold. Janet kissed each in turn, noticing again how Elizabeth affectionately threw her arms around her neck whereas Mary merely pecked at the part of her chin unencumbered with hairs. After wishing them goodnight she picked up the lamp and made her way along the draughty corridors to her own room, mercifully sheltered against the worst of the blast in the north wing.

Within a few minutes Mary was asleep, but Elizabeth kept staring into the darkness of the canopy, listening to the wind roaring past the window. She was thinking about her cove, a secret place which not even Mary knew about, a sand-encroached cleft in the rocks near Pwll Dafan which was her hiding place for all the shells and brightly-coloured pebbles she collected from the beach. She shared most things with Mary: primrose and violet chains in the spring, garlands of bluebell and harebell in the summer, blackberries and bilberries in the autumn; but not her cove. Mary had no patience with her passion for beach things and had once broken two of her best hermit-crab shells. Perhaps the waves were pounding over her treasures now as they had done in a previous gale; if so, it was time she found another hiding place further inland, perhaps at Waun y Mer where there was a copse of gorse and elder. She had seen a fox make his den there once and what a fox could do she could also. Her problem partially solved, she turned and settled more comfortably into the feather mattress.

But just as she was dozing off she heard a voice. She listened intently and heard another, louder and more commanding, followed by the clatter of hooves on the cobbles of the yard. She glanced at Mary, who appeared to be asleep, and pulled back the coverlet. Quietly she lowered herself to the floor, went over to the window and peered through the thick whorled panes. At first she could see little, for sleet and foam kept hurtling past in the darkness; but she pressed her nose hard against the glass and eventually made out two figures standing by the stable doors. As she watched the doors opened and, in the flickering light of a lantern she saw the familiar figure of her father, gesticulating and pointing upwards at the loft. Almost immediately a horse and cart were backed into the entrance and several men began throwing boxes and bales on the straw-covered floor. Even before the last box had hit the ground the horse was pulled forward and whipped into a trot down the track leading to the beach. Barely had the sound died away when three mules appeared, their pannier-bags bulging with sacks and strange-shaped bundles. These, too, were thrown into the barn where they were quickly seized and carried into the interior of the building. Now the yard was full of shadowy figures and she could see her father again, angrily exhorting the men to be quick. Mark Edwards appeared for a fleeting moment, directing men staggering under the weight of enormous sacks towards the stable. Then, as though by magic, the yard emptied and the stable doors closed. Elizabeth had a brief glimpse of her father and Mark hurrying off in the direction of the deeply-roaring sea and could see nothing more, however hard she tried; and suddenly she became aware that her feet were icy cold on the bare floor boards. She stayed at the window a little longer but nothing further occurred so she returned to the bed and climbed into its comforting warmth. Mary was still fast asleep.

She lay on her back for a while, wondering. There was no doubt about it now. A wreck had occurred and her father was directing the rescue of cargo and sailors. As long as he was there all would be well, and in the morning he would regale Mary and her with stories of all that had happened during the night. Then they would all go down to the beach and see the ship and the poor sailors, who no doubt would be helped by her prayers. Comforted by these thoughts she fell asleep and did not wake until the first faint light of dawn was filtering through the window.

Elizabeth dressed quickly, finishing even before Mary, and rushed downstairs to the banqueting room where her father usually breakfasted alone, but there was no sign of him. Disappointed, she went to the kitchen, only to find that Mary was already sitting at the table, scooping up her oatmeal porridge. Mary brandished the spoon at her.

"If you're not ready soon I'm going to the beach without you."

"Oh, no you're not," said Janet, emerging from the larder carrying a mixing bowl. "You're not going anywhere without Elizabeth. She'll only run after you. Anyway, I don't think I ought to let either of you go in this wind."

"Oh, we'll be all right," said Mary petulantly. "Father said we could go."

"Then eat your breakfasts and I'll wrap you up properly. You're not going out without plenty of good clothing on."

Pouting, Mary set to again with the porridge and Elizabeth did likewise. When they had finished Janet produced their heavy winter coats, bonnets and two enormous shawls.

"Come on—I'm not having you catching colds."

She helped the girls into their coats, pulled the bonnets hard down on their heads and wrapped the shawls around them until only their eyes were showing.

"There! Now take care down that old beach. Look after your sister, Mary."

"Of course I'll look after her," said Mary. "Come on, Elizabeth, I'll race you."

They ran out through the porch, crossed the yard and started down the path to the beach. There they had to slow down for, although it had stopped sleeting, the wind was still gusting strong enough to make them bend almost double. They struggled on but had only just left the shelter of the perimeter wall when two men came towards them, swaying as though drunk and each carrying a small keg. As they got nearer one of them dropped back slightly then suddenly pulled a club from his pocket and felled the other with a wild, looping blow. Laughing shrilly, he picked up his victim's keg and went loping off over the fields. Mary grasped Elizabeth's hand and pulled her in a wide circuit around the inert, groaning figure, but before they could regain the path they were confronted by another ruffian, singing loudly and brandishing two bottles. As soon as he saw the girls he raised the bottles in mock salute and put one to his lips. Liquor ran down over his beard and he staggered towards them. This time Elizabeth needed no urging, and both girls ran as fast as they could across the sand dunes, eventually reaching the beach breathless and exhausted. There they paused, eyes watering, staring at the sight that confronted them.

The ship was lying in the middle of the vast expanse of glistening, debris-strewn sand, looking like a black stranded whale. Although now just out of reach of the hissing, rushing surf, she lay on her side with masts and rigging gone and a great, gaping hole in her prow. But what amazed the girls was not the stricken vessel but the huge crowd of people that had gathered around it. There were at least three hundred of them, mostly men but also many women and children, milling, fighting or hacking at the gunwales and keel with axes and adzes. On the steeply sloping deck uniformed men armed with staves were trying to resist attempts to climb aboard, but with little success; and even from that distance the shouts and cries of pain could plainly be heard. Under the jutting stern a smaller group appeared to be building a bonfire of barrels and wreckage, and near them the ship's long-boat was already burning fiercely. Out in the still-broiling sea people were wading, even up to their armpits, trying to salvage a few floating boxes and bales; and not far away several women fought viciously over a length of silk. Watching everything were eight or nine foreign-looking men, huddled together for warmth and safety; and even as the girls stared at them one was struck on the head by a stone hurled by someone on the beach. Mary's grip on Elizabeth's hand tightened.

"Come, Elizabeth. We must look for father."

They skirted the beach, keeping to the bank and dodging several mules and donkeys laden with panniers, until they reached a low rocky promontory jutting out into the sand. There the sight that met them brought them to a sudden frightened halt. On the highest point of the promontory, surrounded by about a dozen of his farm-hands, was their father. Facing them was a shouting, cursing mob of men and youths, many brandishing cudgels and sticks. Because of the wind the girls could not hear what was being said, but they were in no doubt that their father's life was in danger; and when they saw the foremost rank of the crowd surge forward, striking at the farm-hands with fists and weapons, Elizabeth began to cry.

Then, just as it seemed that Isaac and his men were about to be engulfed by the struggling mass of bodies, a loud shouting from the beach brought all activity to a halt. Everyone, attackers and attacked, turned to see a huge plume of black smoke pouring from the ship. Immediately there was cheering and the mob went rushing down the beach, whooping and knocking each other over in their haste. Isaac and the farm-hands watched them for a moment and some of them began to laugh. Amazed and encouraged by such a sudden change of fortune, Mary pulled Elizabeth towards the promontory.

But as they got near it Isaac saw them. His face, smiling a moment ago, changed, and his lips tightened into a hard, ugly line. He pushed a man aside and came towards them.

"What are you two doing here?"

"We've come to see the wreck," said Mary, adding defensively, "You said we could come."

Isaac's complexion reddened.

"I said no such thing," he bawled. "I said I might let you if it was safe. It's not safe. Go back to the house immediately."

"But, father—"

"Go back," roared Isaac. "Go now. This instant. If you don't I'll strap you when I return."

Mary knew better than to argue with her father. Both girls turned and began running along the bank, but before they had gone a dozen paces they stopped, horrified. At their feet, not previously seen in a fold in the ground, were three corpses. Two were almost unrecognisable as human beings, their faces starched with blood; and the third, although unmarked, had great gashes in his clothes, revealing the white, bloated obesity of the drowned. The girls sought to move but could not. Isaac smiled grimly.

"Now will you go home?"

They required no second bidding. Hand in hand, helped by the wind in their backs, they ran as fast as they could, and did not stop until they reached the safety of Janet's kitchen.

CHAPTER 3

ISAAC WILLIAMS' ancient coach rumbled along the track leading from Sker House to the main road connecting Nottage and Kenfig. In it were Isaac, Janet, Mary and Elizabeth. It was late spring but only the girls showed pleasure at the sight of green fields and hedgerows rushing past on either side. Isaac and Janet sat on opposite seats, avoiding each other's gaze, their minds occupied with the business confronting them: the official enquiry into the loss of the French vessel *Le Vainqueur*. Then, just as the coach reached the road and slowed down for the corner, their reverie was interrupted by a loud thumping on the vehicle's sides. They looked up to see two men shaking their fists. Quickly the angry faces disappeared from view as the horses gathered speed, but not before the girls had seen them. They stared wonderingly at their father, but he pretended not to notice. Janet pursed her lips and scowled.

"I told you it was a mistake bringing the children with you. It'll be the same at that court, mark my words."

Isaac scowled back.

"Nonsense, woman. I've already told you—I had to bring them. The magistrates must be made to realise I'm a widower with two children to support—an upholder of the law, not the rogue some people are making me out to be. When they see these two little ones they'll know I'm a good family man."

"And what if they find against you? What'll you do then?"

Isaac stole a quick glance at the girls and was relieved to see that a hovering sparrow-hawk, gliding along at the same speed as the coach, had momentarily distracted their attention.

"There's no danger of that. No one's going to find against me, and as Constable of the Hundred of Newcastle I know how the law works. Anyway, I've a few friends who'll testify on my behalf, so stop carping."

"I hope you're right," said Janet darkly. "For their sakes."

"Oh, for God's sake, woman, I know I'm right. By the time today is over everyone'll know that I acted legitimately and all gossip will be silenced."

He resumed his staring and neither spoke again until the coach drew up on the gravelled courtyard of the Town Hall. There Janet's warning proved correct for, even before the wheels had stopped turning, they were surrounded by a crowd of jostling, shouting people, many of whom also banged on the sides of the vehicle. Wisely the coachman eased the horses forward until they were opposite the main entrance where Isaac leaped out and, with expletives, pushed aside the nearest gesticulating men; and the ones behind, seeing Janet and the children, fell back a little. Glaring contemptuously at them,

Isaac shepherded his charges through the doorway and pushed his way down the courtroom aisle until they found a vacant bench. There they sat, with Elizabeth perched on Janet's knee and Isaac studiously ignoring the stares and mutterings of the people around them. The girls remained silent, awe-stricken by such treatment of their father.

For ten minutes the hubbub went on around them, receding only when the clerk of the court appeared and banged on the floor with his staff. In a high-pitched, reedy voice he called for silence, and when some semblance of order had been achieved three magistrates entered and took up their positions at the table on the dais.

"Be upstanding for Mr. Justice Mackworth," quavered the clerk.

After the noise of rising and re-sitting the court became reasonably still. Mackworth, a florid-faced, heavily built man, stared with dislike at the assembled throng, adjusted his wig and nodded to the clerk.

"Silence!" trilled the clerk. "Pray silence for Mr. Justice Mackworth."

Mackworth glared around again, consulted his numerous documents and began speaking in a low, grating voice.

"As you have been informed by notices posted throughout the parishes this court has been convened to enquire into the wreck of a vessel off Sker in December last in the year of our Lord 1753. It is not a court of justice—already seventeen men have been apprehended in connection with that affair—but more may be added should we discover it necessary this morning. Our main purpose is to look into the subject of the loss of the ship's cargo, which was misappropriated on the night of the wreck and carried away in such quantities that the authorities saw fit to order the reading of notices in the churches of Pyle, Maudlam, Newton-Nottage and Margam, reminding congregations that the plundering of wrecks is a capital offence. Yet in spite of those notices and subsequent searches carried out by constables, very little of the cargo has been recovered. It is to enquire into this matter, and if necessary apprehend further culprits, that we are now sitting. Clerk! Are all the witnesses present?''

"Yes, your honour," said the clerk. "I think they are. I hope so."

"They'd better be," said Mackworth menacingly. "Proceed. Outline the events that occurred."

The clerk spent a few minutes consulting his papers then began reading.

"On the twelfth of December, 1753, a French merchantman by the name of *Le Vainqueur* was bound from Lisbon to Le Havre with a mixed cargo comprising the following: 789 chests of oranges, 650 frails of figs, 84 Brazil planks and an unknown quantity of sacks containing lemons—the ship's log was not always readable because of immersion in sea-water, your honour. There were also a number of kegs of brandy and several baskets containing bottles of port wine, number not known. The vessel had been driven off course by the violent winds and it is thought that the captain mistook St. George's Channel for the English Channel—unfortunately, as you know, sir, he is no longer alive to testify on that score, having been drowned on the night of the tragedy. The vessel quickly broke up on the notorious rocks of Sker and was subsequently driven on to the beach. Of the crew of eleven, eight survived, but the captain and two others were later found dead. They—"

"What did their injuries consist of?" Mackworth interjected suddenly.

"The two deck-hands had their heads stove in, but the captain was merely drowned. There were no marks on his body, but it is thought—"

"Were those injuries consistent with blows or other human agency?"

"It's difficult to tell, sir. The constable who examined the bodies was unsure whether the marks had been caused by being beaten against the rocks or whether they had been inflicted by-er-other means."

"Go on," said Mackworth, suddenly losing interest.

"The captain's body, though unmarked, had been rifled. His clothes had been torn apart and his cabin boy has testified that at the moment of disembarking in the long-boat his master had on his person a purse containing seventeen gold Portugese pieces. Neither purse nor gold has been recovered. In addition, his silver shoe buckles had been torn off and misappropriated, as also had his watch, which has since been recovered from a local watchmaker, to whom it had been taken for repairs. The person concerned in that has already been apprehended—"

"But not the one who took his buckles?"

"No, sir. The buckles are still missing. Almost as soon as the ship struck the reef a number of men gathered around it, later swelling to several hundred as news of the wreck travelled around the neighbourhood. Unfortunately, the constables and excise men did not arrive until dawn, by which time most of the cargo had disappeared—carried off to nearby hamlets or pre-arranged hiding places. Several men were hacking at the ship with axes and taking away planks, rigging and ironwork. Later on it was set on fire with the intention of obtaining valuable nails and bolts. The long-boat suffered a similar fate. Nothing the constables could do restrained them—indeed for a time the officers themselves went in fear for their lives. Even the bailiff was threatened. Very ugly scenes developed until the looters began to accuse each other—"

"Who accused who?" asked Mackworth in a dry voice.

"Many of those present were vociferous against Mr. Isaac Williams and his farm-labourers, accusing them of having already misappropriated most of the cargo and stacking it away in the barns and stables of Sker Manor."

"But the buildings at Sker were searched, were they not?" said Mackworth. "Yet I understand that not a great deal of merchandise was found there."

"Very little indeed, sir, compared with the full tally we know was on the ship."

"Then how do you account for the discrepancy?"

"I cannot, sir. The constables found barely a tenth of the cargo there, and when asked about that Mr. Williams stated that he had salvaged as much as possible to keep it out of the hands of the looters—to guard it until the rightful owners could be notified."

"Did he now?" A ghost of a smile crossed Mackworth's face. "Then what happened to the other nine tenths, pray?"

"I cannot tell you, sir, except to say that shortly after the wreck a great number of oranges, lemons and figs were being sold in the markets of Bridgend and Aberafon—and even as far as Cowbridge."

"At a good price, I'll wager."

"A very good price indeed, I'm told. Considerable profits must have been made by the person or persons who were in a position to . . . store the fruit and then convey it to the markets at a safe and suitable time. The Brazil planks have not been recovered. It is thought that they have been buried somewhere on the dunes to await disposal later."

Mackworth stroked his heavy jaw with stubby fingers.

"But who stored it? Have you been able to ascertain that?"

"No, sir, but it is a well-known fact that Sker House has many hiding places and secret recesses. Anyway, the people on the beach were accusing Mr. Williams and his men of having carried away most of the stuff before they themselves could lay their hands on it. At one stage the constables had to protect Mr. Williams himself, or he would have come to serious harm."

"And is that what the local populace still thinks?"

"They do indeed, sir. I believe Mr. Williams has received many threats since this unfortunate affair, and is greatly disliked in the neighbourhood. Indeed, he often goes in fear of his life."

Mackworth's eyes searched the court for Isaac and found him.

"Does he, indeed? We will question Mr. Williams about that later. At the moment it seems to me we have a case of the pot calling the kettle black—not an unusual occurrence these days. The sooner we call the witnesses the sooner we'll arrive at the truth. Get on with it. Call the first witness."

Flustered, the clerk consulted his list.

"Call Griffith Peregrine."

Griffith Peregrine stepped forward, a short, portly man of about fifty, still wearing his heavy, triple-cloaked top-coat and tricorn. He removed the tricorn, leaving his wig slightly awry and, puffing slightly, climbed into the witness box.

"You are Griffith Peregrine," said the clerk, "of Swansea, in the County of Glamorgan?"

"I am," said Peregrine and repeated the oath in a strong Gloucestershire accent.

"You were present at the scene of the wreck shortly after it occurred?"

"I was."

"Then kindly describe to his honour what you saw."

Peregrine adjusted his cravat, cleared his throat and turned to Mackworth.

"As soon as I heard there was a ship in distress I travelled to Sker with all speed, but I did not reach there until just before dawn. By then it was already too late to save either vessel or cargo. When I arrived at the beach the ship was being hacked to pieces, as you have heard, and tallow and barrels stacked around it with the intention of setting it on fire. I and the constables ordered the people to desist but they paid not the slightest attention, except, of course, to threaten and curse us. I—"

"Then it was an ugly scene," said Mackworth ruminatively.

"Very ugly indeed. I have never before witnessed such contempt for the law. It would have taken a troop of soldiers to stop the miscreants, but unfortunately such was not available."

"And would you say that the position was made worse by the presence of Mr. Isaac Williams and his men?"

"Indeed I do. Considering the size of the ship I expected to see a great deal of merchandise on the beach, instead of which there was very little. I questioned the crew, all of whom stated that during the turmoil of darkness they had seen much stuff taken away, but of course they could not identify those responsible. Then, not long after I arrived, Isaac Williams and a group of men—whom I now know to be his farm-hands— were surrounded by a hostile crowd accusing them of having already taken the lion's share of the cargo, thus leaving very few pickings for themselves."

Mackworth held up a peremptory hand.

"And what was Mr. Williams' attitude to that? Consider your answer carefully before you reply."

Peregrine considered, but not for long.

"He protested his innocence, of course, but he did so in a supercilious grinning manner that further incensed his accusers. If it had not been for the presence of the constables and a diversion caused by the ship going up in flames he would have been man-handled. I believe he later thought it expedient to invite the constables to search Sker farm—"

"Which they did and found very little there. You speak French then, Mr. Peregrine, if you conversed with the crew?"

"I do, sir."

"Then tell me, what did you glean from them?"

"Very little, I'm afraid. They were all distressed, having narrowly escaped death by drowning, and it was a bitter night. In addition they were being threatened by the local rogues, who were still incensed about the cargo and who probably wanted to rob them of their personal possessions, few though they were."

"The captain was robbed, was he not?"

"Indeed he was. It was from the crew that I was able to ascertain the contents of his purse and that he had a watch and a pair of expensive shoe buckles. I found it odious that the survivors were kept on the beach throughout the night without sustenance or shelter of any kind after such an ordeal."

"Two of the crew were also dead, I'm told. Did the survivors say anything to denote that murder had been committed with a view to obtaining the reward for finding dead bodies?''

''No, sir.'' Peregrine sounded rueful. ''I was unable to ascertain that, and my examination of the corpses failed to reveal the true cause of death.''

''A pity. What is your opinion about the cargo, Mr. Peregrine? Do you think that such a great amount could have been hidden somewhere? Say in Sker Manor or its outbuildings?''

Peregrine nodded quickly several times.

''From what I can gather, sir, that is not only possible but very likely. Whoever was first on the scene had ample time to place the merchandise in suitable hiding places—and Mr. Williams and his men were, I believe, first on the scene. Furthermore, I can only reiterate what I heard subsequently—that most of the local populace believe that Isaac Williams took at least three-quarters of the cargo for himself.''

Mackworth picked up a quill and made an entry in a ledger. When he looked up again his eyes were beady.

''Mr. Peregrine, are you biased against Mr. Williams? Has he done you an injury in any way?''

''No, sir,'' said Peregrine, surprised at the question. ''He has done me no injury. I can only speak the truth as I see it.''

''But he is no friend of yours, that is quite obvious. I must remind you that evidence is one thing, hearsay another, and there is too much of the latter in your testimony. Step down, please.''

''But, sir—''

''Step down, Mr. Peregrine,'' said Mackworth harshly. ''Should I think fit I will call you again.''

Amid sympathetic murmuring Peregrine climbed out of the box and resumed his seat. Mackworth fingered the gavel but decided not to use it. He nodded again to the clerk.

''Call Edward Savours,'' called the clerk.

Edward Savours rose from a side bench. Aged about thirty, he was immaculately dressed in a three-quarter length blue satin jacket, white calf-skin trousers and black riding boots with turned-down tops. He took the oath in a cultured English voice, turned to Mackworth and flicked away an imaginary speck of dust from his sleeve with a large, silk handkerchief.

"Mr. Savours," said Mackworth, "at what time did you arrive at the scene of the wreck?"

"Eight-thirty or thereabouts, I would say. My carriage was held up by a fallen tree, or I would have been there sooner. It was just getting light."

"Describe what you saw."

"Well, I must agree, of course, with the description I have just heard. Both ship and long-boat were burning away merrily when I arrived and there was prettly little er—flotsam and jetsam, if that is the right expression, to be seen. I saw little trace of cargo also, except for some bales and boxes that were being taken away by a few of the most ruffianly individuals it has ever been my misfortune to behold. There was also a great deal of drunkenness. I understand that the cargo consisted mainly of citrus fruit, but there must have been a fair quantity of intoxicating liquor, too, if the evidence of my eyes is to be believed. But having said that I must tell you now that I am of the opinion that a wrong construction has been placed on the evidence I have heard so far."

"Oh!" Mackworth sat forward as though he had been pricked from behind. "What d'you mean—that a wrong construction has been placed on the evidence so far?"

"Well—" Again Savours flicked the handkerchief, "—if there was pillaging and looting it was being done, as far as I could make out, by the local cut-throats themselves. Many of them were up to their armpits in the water, seizing the odd bale or sack that floated to shore, and then handing them to accomplices. Mr. Williams, on the other hand, was merely looking on, as helpless as I and the constables. Some of the ring-leaders were whipping up a fury against him, accusing him of having already taken most of the cargo; and I must say I found that very droll coming from the likes of the men I saw there that day."

Mackworth sank back again, still staring at Savours.

"In that case, what have you to say about the previous witness's assertion that Mr. Williams had indeed taken the lion's share of the cargo?"

"Well, of course he had, hadn't he? I questioned him about it and he readily admitted it, pointing out what would have happened to the merchandise if he had not interceded. And I must say, having witnessed with my own eyes what was happening, he was quite correct. If he had not acted as he did not a bale, not a box, would have been recovered. Of that I am quite sure. I was there and—"

He got no further. A sustained outburst of boo-ing and shouting drowned his words, quelled only after Mackworth had repeatedly wielded the gavel.

"Mr. Savours," said Mackworth when he was able to make his voice heard, "you have heard the effect of your statement. I must ask you to consider your words carefully—and I must remind you that barely a tenth of the cargo was recovered from Sker Manor. What then, in your opinion, happened to the rest?"

Savours stared around the courtroom before replying.

"I've no idea. Probably it was carried away by the looters or sank to the bottom of the sea. All I can say is that if Mr. Williams had not acted as he did not a shred of the stuff would have been—"

This time the court erupted in noise. Mackworth banged with the gavel until splinters flew off the table, but it was several minutes before order was restored. Then he bellowed like a bull.

"Silence! Any more of that and I'll clear the court. I will not stand for any interruption. Constables! Keep an eye on the offenders and arrest anyone you see as much as opening their mouths."

His words had the desired effect. Intimidated by eight constables stationing themselves at strategic points the courtroom became reasonably quiet. Mackworth turned again to Savours, a crafty look in his eyes.

"Now, Mr. Savours, I am going to ask you a personal question and I want you to consider carefully before you reply. Tell me this. Are you in any way connected with Mr. Isaac Williams?"

Savours blinked.

"No, I am not."

"Then are you connected with a Mr. John Curre of Monmouth?"

"Not connected although I know him well. I have—carried out certain legal tasks for him."

"Legal tasks, eh! And is it not a fact that Mr. John Curre is related by marriage to Mr. Isaac Williams?"

"Yes, I believe that to be true."

"Furthermore, is not the said Mr. Curre the owner of the estate on which Sker Manor is situated?"

Savours swallowed nervously several times.

"Yes. That is true also."

For a full half minute there was complete silence, then a toothless old woman shouted: "Well done, Mackworth, now you're getting somewhere!" Her words were followed by laughter and cheering and Mackworth, instead of looking angry, smiled impishly, pleased at his ostentatious show of impartiality. But when he spoke his voice was still harsh.

"I must state my belief—and I wish it recorded—that we have here yet another biased witness, reinforcing my view that we will not get to the bottom of this matter until we hear the evidence of Mr. Isaac Williams himself, who seems to be at the centre of the affair. I do not intend to sit here all the morning listening to hearsay and conjecture. Call Isaac Williams."

Isaac stood up among cat-calls and jeers. Janet lowered Elizabeth into his place to reserve it, and immediately the girl's attention was drawn to the person sitting next to her, a good-looking, dark-haired man of about twenty-five. On his lap was a small harp, decorated in a gold-leaf flower motif, very similar to the one her mother had once played. The man saw Elizabeth staring at the harp and smiled, and Elizabeth smiled back. Then she heard her father's voice and craned her neck so that she could see him in the witness box.

"Yes, your honour," Isaac was saying. "It is true that Mr. John Curre is the owner of my estate and that I am related to him, but surely that has no bearing on the matter, Mr. Savours has spoken the truth. At no point did I take any of the cargo for my own personal use, or with the intention of keeping it for future gain. Having lived at Sker for many years I am fully conversant with the attitude of local people towards wrecks and have witnessed on many occasions how their avarice causes them to behave in a vicious and unlawful manner. They regard everything washed ashore as their own personal property, to be fought over and taken away, and the devil take the hindmost. Knowing this I deemed it my duty to safeguard the cargo, ordering my men to take as much as they could to the safe confines of my farm. We were stopped only by the hordes who soon arrived and accused me of having misappropriated the greater part of the merchandise. As you have heard, the constables had to protect me. I—"

"Stop, Mr. Williams, stop!" cried Mackworth. "You are going too quickly for me. Just tell me this. Did you yourself ask the constables to search your premises?"

"I did indeed. Some of the scoundrels were so vociferous that I deemed such a course was the best way of keeping the peace."

"But surely you are aware of the fact that only a tenth of the accountable cargo was found at Sker. What happened to the other nine tenths, pray? Not much has been recovered from the seventeen men already apprehended."

"I've no idea, your honour."

"Could it be that you showed the constables only a part of what you had er-safeguarded? We have heard that Sker House has many hiding places. Had you secreted the greater portion in places you knew the constables could not find?"

Isaac's face filled with righteous indignation.

"No, sir. That is a calumny invented by my enemies."

"Then how do you account for the missing property?"

"I cannot account for it unless it was taken by men other than my own."

"But these other men that you speak of—the horde on the beach—they are the very ones who were accusing you—still are accusing you—of having stolen the cargo. They would hardly do that if there had been sufficient pickings for themselves, would they? Can you explain that?"

"I cannot, except by saying that some of those men are my enemies."

"Your enemies? Why are they your enemies, Mr. Williams?"

Isaac took a deep breath, pleased at the chance of launching his carefully prepared statement.

"Well, sir, you know very well yourself that if you try and do good for the common cause and uphold the law you are bound to make enemies. The looters—or would-be looters—knew that I had prevented them from taking what they regarded as theirs by right, and so they were indignant about it. In addition many of them were drunk and not in full possession of their faculties. They—"

"But they've had plenty of time to sober up since then, haven't they," interrupted Mackworth, "and yet I understand that many in the neighbourhood still threaten you."

"That is so, but you must remember, sir, that I am also Constable of the Hundred of Newcastle. In that position I have had to deal with many miscreants, and as your honour probably knows I have a name for strictness as well as impartiality. The relatives of some of the wrong-doers I have sentenced were in that mob on the beach, and I believe it was they who were stirring up feeling against me. And today, as you can tell from their demeanour, they are still trying to do so. They would do me great harm if they could, in spite of the fact that I am a widower with two small children to support. Farming at Sker is difficult enough as it is, what with the wind and the encroaching sand—"

Mackworth, who had begun to make notes, waved his quill without looking up.

"Have a care, Mr. Williams, or some will say that you try to augment your income by means other than farming."

Isaac saw his mistake and reddened; and before he could recover Mackworth went on:

"Tell me, Mr. Williams, have you any idea as to how some of the crew met their death?"

Isaac shook his head, puzzled and annoyed that he had been stopped elaborating his defence.

"I only know that they were drowned and battered against the rocks."

"Were they drowned first and then battered, or vice versa?"

"I cannot swear to that. All I know is that I saw the captain's body being washed ashore. Indeed, I ordered my men to retrieve the corpse and place it on the sand dunes alongside the other two."

"Was that before the main body of people arrived?"

"It was."

"Then might it have been your own men who robbed the master of his possessions?"

"No. That is impossible. The captain's clothes had not been rifled when I found him. That must have been done later after the crowd had gathered. It was only after the constables arrived that we found he had been robbed."

"And yet you kept the surviving members of the crew on the beach all night. Would it not have been a Christian-like act to have given them shelter, well knowing the ordeal they had been through?"

Isaac snorted.

"Are we not at war with the French, sir, or very nearly so? We are already fighting them in America and India and I understand that full hostilities may break out at any moment. I treated them as enemy aliens."

"But even as enemy aliens they were hardly a menace to you that night, surely?"

"That is true, but with war in the offing who could tell what mischief they might have done. They could have made plans of the vicinity which would help the French considerably should they wish to invade.''

Mackworth opened his mouth to say something more, but before he could do so a man at the back shouted: ''You'll never trap Isaac Williams, Mackworth. He'll wriggle out of anything, you watch.'' Immediately two constables converged in the direction of the voice and there was a short, sharp scuffle. Mackworth stared at Isaac, obviously uneasy and undecided, then he conferred with his fellow magistrates, who nodded several times. After a while Mackworth began speaking in a low, monotonous voice.

''So far we have been unable to ascertain what happened to the missing cargo, but it is our intention to go on with this enquiry until we get to the truth of the matter. The pillaging of wrecks is rife on this part of the coast and must be stopped, and those responsible, whether they are of low birth or high, must be punished. What I want to know is . . . ''

He droned on, making everybody restless; and Elizabeth, who had been watching her father, turned to look again at the man sitting beside her. She leaned forward to have a closer look at the harp and was surprised to see that the intricately entwined flowers were daffodils, not roses like her mother's instrument. Seeing her interest the man smiled, put a finger to his lips, then reached down and plucked a string. A faint but quite audible note sounded in the courtroom, making the people nearest them turn and stare. The man laughed, making Elizabeth laugh too; then Janet, thinking that Elizabeth was the culprit, picked her up and dumped her none too gently on her lap. Not to be outdone Elizabeth took several sly peeps at the stranger, although now he was staring straight in front of him, listening intently to what was being said.

She did not know that this was her first meeting with Thomas Evans, the harpist of Newton, or that the proceedings in the courtroom would one day affect both their lives.

INTERMEZZO

CHAPTER 1

THE INSIDE PASSENGERS of the London-Carmarthen stage coach waited patiently for Elizabeth Williams to sit down. She was leaning perilously out of the window as the vehicle thundered down Sturmi's Common, for it was there, she had informed them, that she would obtain her first glimpse of the sea after a vacation in London.

As on all such long and dangerous journeys, a degree of comradeship had developed, the travellers conversing freely until they knew each other's business. The men, much to the disgust of an elderly spinster occupying a corner seat, were particularly interested in Elizabeth, for she was beautiful and possessed a happy, ingenuous nature that brought out all their protective instincts. They plied her with questions, overt and indirect, until they knew much about her. They discovered that she was nineteen years old, the younger daughter of Isaac Williams, the tenant of Sker Manor, who had sent her and her sister to London in the hope that they would meet affluent suitors. The young ladies had stayed with a rich, widowed aunt who had shown them all the interesting places and introduced them to many well-connected young men, including a member of the aristocracy; but Elizabeth had soon tired of the dirt and summer heat of the city and was returning to Sker, where the air was always fresh and pure, leaving the sister behind to make a good match if she could. As a result she was unsure of the welcome she would receive from her father who, because he found farming a large estate difficult on such an exposed part of the coast, was anxious for his daughters to marry well.

Armed with such interesting information the men had taken Elizabeth to their hearts and so, as the horses lapsed into a canter at the bottom of the hill, and she sat down again, they all stared expectantly at her.

"Well," said the farmer from Gorseinon, who had spent the last few minutes pleasurably studying Elizabeth's shapely, silk-clad bottom. "Did you see it?"

"Oh yes," cried Elizabeth. It's almost blue. But it always is on a day like this, of course."

"Then it won't be long before you'll be home," said the Swansea cornmerchant, beaming.

"No, not long now. I do hope my father has sent the carriage to meet me."

"Oh, he will have done," said the vicar with the heavy certainty of his calling. "Have no fear about that."

But his words could not prevent her jumping up again and leaning out as the coach clattered over the cobbles of Pyle. She scanned the forecourt of the staging inn and saw what she had hoped for: the family carriage with Dafydd Hywel, the groom, leaning against a shaft, a straw in his mouth. She waved and Dafydd was opening the door for her almost before the coach stopped. She said goodbye to the other passengers, who expressed sorrow at losing her, pointed out her boxes and portmanteau to Dafydd, and climbed into the mildewy interior of the carriage.

"Where's my father?" she called as Dafydd shut the door. "Is he at home?"

"Not that I know of," said Dafydd, removing his straw for a moment. "He's away somewhere on business, so he sent me. Janet's getting a meal ready for you."

Elizabeth breathed a sigh of relief. The longer the meeting was postponed the better; now she had a little more time to frame her excuses. Her father would be angry, she knew, especially as she had come without Mary; but Mary liked it in London and would no doubt obey instructions and obtain a husband who would provide her with a good dowry, one that would help the family finances. Well, let Mary provide for them; all she wanted was to walk freely again on the moors and beaches of Sker and never again would she leave home, except for short visits. Certainly she would never again go to London. With such thoughts she settled back more comfortably in the seat, ready to enjoy the final run home.

Soon the carriage was rattling past Marlas farm, and already the air seemed fresher with the tang of salt. As they climbed out of the hollow she could see the sand-dunes, mile upon mile of them, extending into the distance as far as the coast-line; but as they breasted the ridge her joy was tempered by the sight of Maudlam church on its little hill. There her mother was buried, and she remembered that she had not tended the grave since before Christmas; now, probably, it was overrun with weeds and brambles. At the first opportunity she would go and tidy everything up. Only she and Mary did it now. Her father never went near there.

Then they were passing the Town Hall. Grey and forbidding, even on a warm summer afternoon, it intensified her thoughts about her father. It was there that he had been arraigned for plundering and murder eleven years ago. True he had been exonerated and the court could find no evidence against him, but the trial had left its mark on him. Ever since then he had been moody and irritable, with frequent outbursts of violent and uncontrollable temper, and it was a well-known fact that the people in the neighbourhood still hated him, believing him guilty of crimes they themselves tolerated in others. Perhaps that was why he had not married again. Perhaps no woman would have him, not a genteel woman, that is, for slander went far afield. Not that she and Mary minded. A new mistress at Sker might have curtailed their liberty, something a long procession of governesses and tutors had failed to do, and it seemed unlikely that Isaac would marry again now. There was always the possibility, but she would meet that when it came. In the meantime, with tact and astuteness, she could still usually handle him, although the task was becoming increasingly difficult these days.

After fifteen minutes of fairly sedate travel across the gorse-strewn moor, a bumping and swaying told her that the carriage had left the road and was on the track leading to Sker

House. She leaned forward to see its tall, gaunt structure, then smoothed down the dress Aunt Helen had given her and glanced at her face in a small hand mirror. Never was she more pleased that a journey was over.

With a creaking of harnesses the carriage entered the yard and came to a halt near the porch. Elizabeth jumped out, looked at the sea and took several long, deep breaths. Then, gathering up her new dress to protect it from the dirt, she rushed into the house and pushed open the door of the kitchen. As expected, Janet was there, arms deep in a bowl of flour.

"I'm home," shouted Elizabeth. "Oh, Janet! There's nice to see you after all this time." She ran to the housekeeper and threw her arms around her.

Janet did not know whether to laugh or cry.

"Oh, diawch, there's nice to see you, too, merch fach." She wiped her arms in a cloth. "But why have you come alone? Why did you leave your sister in London?"

"Oh, she likes it there. She's staying on for another month or two."

"But didn't you?"

"Well enough, I suppose, for a while. Aunt Helen was very kind to us. We went to all sorts of balls and banquets—saw all the sights—but three months of London was enough for me. It's so dirty and smelly there at this time of the year. I couldn't wait to see the sea and the dunes again, and to hear the birds, so that's why I came without Mary. Oh, Janet! I don't think I'll ever want to leave here again. Where's father?"

"He's gone to Neath on some business. He had your letter saying you'd be back but there was something important he had to attend to. I'm expecting him home sometime tomorrow. He—" Janet broke off as Dafydd came in and deposited the luggage on the floor. "—he doesn't like it that you've come on your own, though. He was quite angry when he read your letter. But I don't suppose it will bother him too much—he's away a lot himself these days."

"Oh, he'll understand when I tell him how much I wanted to come home. Look, Janet. How do you like my dress? Aunt Helen bought it for me." Elizabeth whirled round, flouncing out the skirt. "It's the latest fashion and I've two more just as good. Wasn't that kind of her? Oh! and I've brought a present for you, too—one I'm sure you'll like so you must see it now."

She rushed forward, seized a cloth-covered parcel and gave it to Janet, who wiped her hands again before taking it. Slowly and delightedly she unwrapped it to reveal a large, embroidered shawl.

"Oh, cariad! You shouldn't have done this. It's too good for me."

"Nonsense. Nothing's too good for you. Do you like it?"

Janet placed the shawl on her shoulders.

"It's beautiful. But you shouldn't have spent your money on me. I'm too old for such lovely things. But I'll treasure it all the rest of my days."

"Oh, no you don't!" Elizabeth laughed. "There's no putting that away in a drawer for the moths. I want you to wear it every day. Perhaps not in the kitchen but whenever you go out or we've got visitors. You must promise me that."

Janet fingered the shawl.

"Bless you, Elizabeth. Perhaps I shouldn't say this but you were always the generous one. Mary's a nice girl, too, of course, but well—" she blew her nose in a rag; "—off you go and change now. You must be very tired and dirty after your journey. I've made your favourite for you—Welsh cakes, with the best currants from Spain."

Elizabeth sniffed the air.

"And by the smell you're making bara brith, too. Oh, thank you, Janet. I haven't tasted real bread since I've been away—not like yours, anyway. But before I change I must go down to the beach. I can't tell you how much I've wanted to feel the sand under my feet and smell salt air again—and I never thought I'd miss the sound of seagulls so much. I shan't be long. Only half an hour and then I'll come back and tell you all about London. And by then I'll have an appetite big enough to eat everything you've made for me."

She ran towards the door. Janet carefully folded the shawl and replaced it in the wrapping.

"Half an hour, then, and I'll brew a pot of tea. But no longer. I want to hear about all those balls and banquets you've been to."

Elizabeth laughed again and went out into the bright sunlight. She stood for a moment by the porch, admiring the nearby fields of ripening corn, then started down the track to the beach. She picked her way across the rocky hinterland and made straight for her childhood cove near Pwll Dafan. To her surprise she found it almost completely engulfed in soft, yellow sand, probably as a result of the high spring tides, and the surrounding rocks were festooned with bladder wrack, still fresh and shining. She tore off a frond and squeezed the pods, making popping noises. Then she clambered across the rough, jagged ridges to the beach, which was deserted, with not even a fisherman or seaweed gatherer in sight. Next she examined her favourite rock-pool where there had once been a huge dogfish, then skirted the gently-tumbling wavelets, keeping an eye open for unusual shells or pebbles. But the only thing she could find were mussel beds and pieces of driftwood; even the large stump of wood that had marked the last resting place of *Le Vainqueur* had disappeared. The scene was so tranquil and restful it was difficult to remember that such a terrible wreck had occurred there.

Then, just as she was about to retrace her footsteps, still visible in the wet sand, she heard a strange sound, almost as though the strings of a harp had been plucked; but she dismissed that as unlikely in such a deserted place. Intrigued, she walked towards its source, which seemed to be somewhere near a wall above the embankment, and heard it again. There was no mistaking it this time: it was a harp; and as she mounted the grassy verge she saw a man sitting with his back to the wall, the instrument in his lap. As she watched he started to hum softly and, after adjusting a string, he began to sing 'Dafydd y Garreg Wen' in Welsh. Elizabeth listened, enthralled by the rich tenor voice, marvelling at the way it blended with the delicate, tremulous notes of the harp. Pure and clear the words came to her, and she felt strangely moved. She had heard the song many times before, but never so beautifully rendered, and the pathos of the air went straight to her heart, making her feel sad yet exhilarated.

But in mid-note the singer saw her. He stared at her, the cadence strangled at birth.

"Oh, please don't stop," said Elizabeth. "I was enjoying listening to you."

"Were you?" He gave a faint smile, but still seemed unsure of himself. "I didn't know anybody was there."

"I'm sorry if I disturbed you. I heard you from the beach and I had to come and listen. Was that 'David of the White Rock' you were singing? It's one of my favourite songs."

"Yes, it was. I'm glad you like it. It's one of mine, too."

"It's such a lovely air. Can you sing it in English as well as in Welsh?"

"I can sing in Welsh and in English."

Elizabeth went nearer him, noting the strong but delicate hands, still holding the harp, and the dark, good-looking face with brown, still-distrustful eyes.

"Why are you out here on your own? You should have a proper audience, not just the sea."

He laughed.

"The sea is a very good audience. Anyway I'll have a proper one tonight. I'm singing at the Gŵyl Mabsant at the Town Hall in Kenfig. That's why I'm here now—practising for it."

She studied him with renewed interest.

"Then are you Thomas Evans, the harpist from Newton?"

"At your service, ma'am."

He stood up and bowed. Elizabeth felt a stab of excitement. Thomas Evans was well known, a celebrity in musical circles.

"Oh, I'm so glad to have met you, Mr. Evans. I've heard such a lot about you. But the reports do not do you justice.

Your voice is even more beautiful than I imagined."

He bowed again.

"Thank you. It is indeed kind of you to say so. May I ask who I have the honour of addressing?"

"I'm Elizabeth Williams. My father is Isaac Williams of Sker Manor." She nodded in the direction of the house.

"Ah!" the dark eyes flickered. "Then I've had the pleasure of meeting you, I believe."

She frowned.

"You've already met me? I don't recollect that."

"I'm not surprised. It was a long time ago—eleven years to be precise. You were sitting on your housekeeper's knee at the enquiry into the loss of a vessel called *Le Vainqueur*."

Slowly a blush spread across Elizabeth's face. She hated to be reminded of the episode, even now.

"Oh, that!" she said with feigned indifference. "Yes, I do remember being at the enquiry but I don't recall seeing you there. Of course, I was very young at the time. I couldn't have been more than seven or eight—"

"You were more interested in my harp than me. You kept looking at it as though you were bewitched by it."

"Did I? I don't recollect that, I'm afraid. You must have a very good memory, Mr. Evans."

"No need for a good memory as far as you were concerned, Miss Williams. You were such a pretty little girl; and then, of course, there was that business of the—" He broke off suddenly, embarrassed.

"What business?" asked Elizabeth quickly.

"Well—the enquiry itself, I mean. I was sorry for you stuck in that stuffy courtroom with all that legal jargon going on. Your sister too. I kept wondering why you'd been brought there."

"I don't remember much about it," said Elizabeth defensively. "I know it was an unhappy time. My father was being arraigned for something he hadn't done."

"Ye-es. I believe it was something like that. But he was exonerated, wasn't he? And that's the important thing.

Anyway, it's a long time ago. Most people have forgotten all about it."

"I doubt it. There are still some who bear him a grudge and think him guilty in some way."

"We-ell, it's all water under the bridge now, isn't it? Finished and done with. You were a very good little girl, I remember. You didn't fidget much. Your sister was much worse than you. She was hardly still for a minute. Where is she now, by the way?"

"She's in London."

"In London! Now that's a place I'd like to visit."

Elizabeth smiled, grateful for the sudden change of subject.

"Visit perhaps, and then return. I've just come back from there and very glad to do so. It's dirty and smells abominably at this time of year."

"Maybe so, but I'd like to go there, all the same. All the best musicians work there. That's the place to go to if you want to get on."

"Oh, well, I can understand your desire from that point of view, but perhaps your voice would not be quite so good in such polluted air. And I doubt if 'Dafydd y Garreg Wen' would sound as nice in London as it does out here on Sker beach."

"Then I shall consult you before taking up an appointment there."

They both laughed.

"I wonder," said Elizabeth appraising him, "if I may ask you a great favour. Would you sing another verse of 'Dafydd y Garreg Wen' for me? I did so enjoy listening to you."

Thomas picked up the harp as though to oblige then glanced up at the sun.

"Willingly, Miss Williams, but I regret not now. I was on the point of leaving when you appeared—I have to meet Eifion Philips, the fiddler, at the Town Hall. I'm late now and we have to arrange the programme. He gets annoyed if I'm not on time. But if you really want to hear me sing why don't you come tonight. If you like 'Dafydd y Garreg Wen' so much I'll sing it again, specially for you."

"Oh, would you?" Her brow puckered as she weighed the possibility. "But I don't know whether I can come. I've so many things to do. I've only just got back from London—"

"It's a very special Mabsant," he said coaxingly, "in honour of St. Mary Magdalen, the patron saint of Maudlam, so many respectable people will be there: well-to-do people, so you won't feel out of place, I'm quite sure of that."

"Well—I don't know—"

"It starts at seven. I'm sure you could come if you wanted to. I'm singing a new song, too—one I think you'd like. It's better than 'Dafydd y Garreg Wen'.

"Better than 'Dafydd y Garreg Wen'? Then it must be good."

"Then come and hear it for yourself and let me know which you prefer."

She turned and began walking in the direction of the house.

"I'll see. I can't promise anything."

"You'll enjoy the dancing, too," he called after her. "Eifion Philips is the best fiddler around these parts."

"I'm sure of that," she said over her shoulder, "otherwise you wouldn't be playing with him. Perhaps. I'll think about it."

He watched her until she was out of sight then shouldered the harp and set off across the moor, trying to keep his mind on the parts he had been practising all the afternoon; but with every step he thought about his encounter with Elizabeth Williams. Although he remembered her as a particularly attractive child he had been startled by her beauty. Now, with her long fair hair, blue eyes and well-proportioned body she was enough to turn any man's head. But what had surprised him most was her friendly, happy demeanour. There was no aristocratic nonsense about her in spite of her superior upbringing; and she had said she liked his voice.

Without slackening his stride he unslung the harp and went through 'Dafydd y Garreg Wen' again, from beginning to end.

CHAPTER 2

BY EIGHT O'CLOCK the mabsant was in full swing. The main room of the Town Hall, previously the scene of the enquiry, was crowded with couples dancing a jig to the accompaniment of Eifion Philips, fiddling so furiously he was sometimes in danger of falling off the dais. Sitting on benches around the walls were older women, knitting, smoking pipes or making surreptitious remarks about the dancers. At one end of the room a group of dandies laughed and joked; at the other several farm workers in their Sunday clothes eyed possible partners and fortified their courage with ale from a battery of casks. From the vantage point of a stool on the dais Thomas Evans watched the whirling throng, one foot beating time to the music. Occasionally he glanced at the door, wondering if Elizabeth Williams would come. How old was she now? Nineteen? Twenty? Whatever it was she was a mature woman. She had sounded genuine in wanting to hear 'Dafydd y Garreg Wen' again, too, which meant that she would probably like 'Bugeilio'r Gwenith Gwyn' which was sweeping the valleys at that time. But it would be foolish to expect her to come to a village function just to hear him sing a popular ballad. A ball at Nottage Court was more to her liking, for she was a member of the *crachach*, after all. On the other hand if she did come he knew he would sing well and vaguely he wondered why. It was just conceit: he wanted to impress a handsome, well-connected girl. The sooner he stopped having silly thoughts the better.

Then he saw her, standing by the door, wearing a blue dress that exactly matched the colour of her eyes. She was being jostled by a crowd of men carrying pots of ale, so he leaped to his feet and went to her rescue.

"I'm so glad you could come."

She managed to avoid a hovering tankard.

"I'm sorry I'm late. I had several things to do and this dress had to be altered at the last moment."

"It's a very beautiful dress. The most beautiful I've seen."

"Thank you." She smiled gratefully at him. "I'm glad you like it. I don't feel quite comfortable in it yet, but I expect I will in time."

He took her arm and guided her away from the danger area near the door.

"Can I get you something to eat? Or drink perhaps? Or would you rather dance?"

"Oh, I haven't long eaten. I think I'd prefer to dance. I love dancing."

Feeling both elated and nervous he put his arms around her, waited for a gap and then led her among the gyrating couples. Elizabeth danced gracefully and well, and he knew that he would have to concentrate hard to keep up with her. Soon they were breathless and laughing like everyone else, and when eventually the music stopped she clung to him, her face flushed and happy.

"Oh, I did enjoy that. I haven't danced a jig for ages."

"In that case you danced very well, Miss Williams. You must have had a great deal of practice in the past."

"I did quite a lot in London, but not a jig. They prefer more stately dances there."

"Well, perhaps we can arrange a stately one for you later."

With the other perspiring dancers they turned expectantly to Eifion Philips, now in his role of Master of Ceremonies, who was making loud clearing noises in his throat.

"Ladies and gentlemen, you've been at it for over an hour now. It's time some of you had a rest. I can see that the legs of some of you are beginning to buckle at the knees—"

He paused for the expected shouts of "Nonsense" and "Get on with it" to die away.

"Not now. Later. There's someone here you've all been waiting for—indeed I know some of you came just to hear him. You will not be disappointed. Ladies and gentlemen, order please for your own renowned singer and harpist, who will perform the first of six songs for you tonight, beginning with a very special one—one that's all the rage at the moment but not yet heard down here. Silence, please, for Thomas Evans."

There was an outburst of clapping and Thomas looked shyly at Elizabeth.

"This is the one I was telling you about. I hope you like it. May I dance with you again later?"

"Of course." She placed a hand on his arm. "I'm so looking forward to hearing you sing."

He climbed on the stage, picked up the harp and gave it a trial strum, although he knew that every string had been perfectly tuned. Then, looking directly at Elizabeth, he said:

"This is a new song as Eifion has told you, ladies and gentlemen. It's about the love of a man for a woman in a higher position in life than he is. Some say it's based on a true experience. I can't vouch for that, not knowing the author, but it's a good song and I know you'll like it. It's called 'Bugeilio'r Gwenith Gwyn'."

He began hesitantly, for it was the first time he had sung the air in public, and he felt nervous; moreover he wanted to impress Elizabeth; but after the first few bars he knew he was in good voice and that the long hours spent rehearsing the beautiful, plaintive melody would stand him in good stead. Soon he was enjoying himself, blending perfectly with the notes of the harp, and quick glances at the sea of faces told him that everyone was listening with rapt attention, especially Elizabeth, who was staring at him with lips slightly parted, as enthralled as anyone. He sang the verses alternately in Welsh and English, and when eventually the last lingering note died away there was loud applause. Delighted with the song's reception, and pleased that Elizabeth was clapping louder than anyone, he bowed several times.

"There! I told you you'd like it, didn't I?"

The applause became tumultuous, but he waited for it to die down then held up a hand.

"No more for now, ladies and gentlemen. Eifion has a full programme and won't be pleased if I go out of turn—but I'll sing it again for you later, if you like, together with another song that's been specially requested by a lady."

Amid cries of "Encore" and "See that you do" he returned to Elizabeth. She looked at him with shining eyes.

"That was marvellous. You sang it beautifully. It's a lovely song."

"Thank you. Did you like it better than 'Dafydd y Garreg Wen'?"

"Yes, I think so. But I'd like to hear both again to make sure."

"So you shall." Then, as Eifion launched into a reel he added: "Would you like to dance again now?"

She took a gaily-painted Spanish fan from her purse and snapped it open.

"Not for the present, if you don't mind. It's so hot in here. Would it be possible to go outside for a short while—just for a little fresh air?"

He nodded and guided her across the crowded floor to the courtyard. There they found other couples of like mind, leaning against the perimeter wall, enjoying the cool, evening air. They walked towards the wall themselves but at that moment Elizabeth caught sight of water gleaming in the moonlight on the other side of the road.

"Oh, look! There's Kenfig Pool. How beautiful it seems tonight. I've never been so close to it at night time before. There's hardly a ripple on the surface. That means there's little chance of hearing the bell, I suppose."

He smiled gravely.

"I doubt if you'll ever hear a bell. It's just a legend. The church isn't under the pool and even if it was you wouldn't hear anything. I mean, it's impossible if you think about it—"

She gave him a mischievous glance.

"Oh, it is possible, surely! I know many people who have heard it."

"Imagination, that's all. Anyway, the city wasn't anywhere near here. It was buried under the dunes—quite a way from the pool." He pointed. "That's what I've been told by a friend who knows the history of the place."

"Then you were told wrong, Thomas. Do you mind if I call you Thomas?"

"No, of course not. Most people do."

"And I'd prefer if you called me Elizabeth. Now then Thomas, I have every respect for your learned friend but he's talking nonsense. Of course the church is under the water. The top of the steeple can be seen quite easily on a clear day—many have told me so. You can even see the tops of the houses if you go out in a boat and put your eyes close to the water."

"Imagination again. All you can see are reeds moving below the surface. They make strange shadows. The city was built to the north, as I say, around the old castle over there—"

She fanned her face rapidly in mock anger.

"Oh, dear! I don't know what to do with a man like you, Thomas. I thought all musicians were romantic people. You're trying to spoil such a beautiful legend. I tell you what! Let's walk down as far as the water's edge and listen. Then, if we hear a bell, even faintly, you'll have to eat your own words, won't you?"

His smile changed to an indulgent grin.

"Very well. If we hear anything resembling a bell I'll eat my words."

They crossed the road, went through a gate and entered a gorse-lined path so rough and uneven she had to cling to his arm for support. They reached the pool, skirted its edge and eventually came to a stile. Without hesitation Elizabeth climbed on the topmost rung and spread out her dress.

"We'll stay here a moment. I'm sure we'll hear something quite soon."

Obediently Thomas remained motionless, pretending to listen. After a while Elizabeth shook her head.

"No, I'm afraid not. I must confess I don't hear anything remotely resembling a bell. Perhaps it's too calm. There's not enough wind. But I won't give up—not yet, anyway. I'd dearly like to prove you wrong. In the meantime, Thomas, tell me again: what was the name of that song you sang tonight?"

"Bugeilio'r Gwenith Gwyn—Watching the White Wheat."

"What a strange title for a song! But I think I can see a reason for it. It's a very sad song, isn't it? Several women near me were actually crying and I even saw one man blowing his nose."

"I'm not surprised. It is a sad song."

"That's to be expected, I suppose. Unrequited love is a sad subject."

"Not as sad as love that's not allowed to blossom."

She frowned, digesting his words.

"N-no, I suppose not. Do you compose music as well as singing it, Thomas?"

"I've tried. I've written one or two songs."

"May I hear them one day?"

"Certainly, if you wish, but not until I've finished them. I'm not satisfied with them yet."

"Then I shall look forward to hearing them when you are. Are they love songs?"

"One is."

"I should very much like to hear that. Do you go to many mabsaint?"

"Quite a few. And to nosweithiau llawen."

"Do you sing and play in every one?"

"In many. Sometimes I charge a fee, sometimes I don't. It all depends where they're held. Some of the farming areas aren't too prosperous and can't pay much so I sing just for the pleasure of it."

"That's very generous of you but I trust you do not underrate yourself. With a voice like yours you should command quite large fees."

"I'm not dependent on music for a living. I'm a carpenter by trade. I've a fairly large workshop at Newton."

"So I've heard. What sort of things do you make?"

"Anything that demands wood—furniture, doors, window-frames, coffins—"

"Coffins! Do you make many of those?"

"Too many for my liking. In Newton people die very young or very old. I make many children's coffins."

"Poor little things. That must be a very sad task for you."

"It is, especially as I've known many of the children. Most of them die of a fever."

"Have you ever heard the tolaeth?"

"You mean the knocking noise a carpenter hears at night when there's no-one in his shop. No, I've never heard it. I don't believe it exists—like the bell of Kenfig. They're both superstitions—"

He broke off suddenly as a twig cracked in the undergrowth. They looked round but it was only a couple running past them towards the pool. At the water's edge they embraced, their figures silhouetted against the moonlight. Elizabeth smiled down at him.

"You're not married, are you, Thomas?"

"No."

"Why not? Most men of your age are. How old are you now?"

"Thirty-six."

"Then why have you not married?"

He turned his head to the shadows. Always sensitive about his bachelor state he disliked explaining it away.

"I see no point in marriage unless you can be happy."

"That's true, but some woman must have wanted to marry you, surely."

"One or two, perhaps."

"I thought so. Then you must be hard to please."

"No, I'm not hard to please. If the right woman had come along I wouldn't have hesitated, but she hasn't and so that's that. As it is—"

"As it is you distrust women. Oh yes! I can see that now. That's the fact of the matter, isn't it?"

He shook his head violently.

"No indeed. I'm quite happy in the company of women. All I know is that marriage to the wrong one is purgatory. I've seen enough evidence in my own village to know that."

"Then you agree that marriage to the right person is a good thing? I mean, you're not against marriage as such."

"Oh, no. I've also seen much happiness come from good marriages. It's just my misfortune not to have—not to have—"

"Not to have met the right woman."

"Yes."

She regarded him thoughtfully for a moment.

"I can see I'll have to take you in hand, Thomas. We can't have a handsome man like you, who can sing so beautifully, loose in the single state in the borough of Kenfig. I shall have to think about you most carefully."

He grinned up at her. She was mocking him, but in a gentle way that did not offend.

"Then if you could do something about my parlous condition I would be very grateful. I would willingly leave my single state for the joy of matrimony—to the right person, of course."

"Oh, it will be to the right person, never fear. I will see to that. Now let's be quiet for a moment. I thought I heard a bell."

She turned her head, giving Thomas the opportunity to study her in profile. With the moonlight glinting in her hair she seemed even more beautiful than when he had first met her, and he marvelled that she was out there alone with him, favouring his company more than any other. Suddenly he knew that if he was not careful he might act foolishly so he resolved to be cautious. Then she surprised him by holding out her arms.

"No, Thomas, I don't think we shall hear anything after all, so I won't be able to make you eat your words. But I think we'd better return now. Will you help me down, please?"

He reached up to support her, but as she climbed down she stumbled on the uneven ground and fell against him, her hands on his shoulders. Her eyes were mischievous.

"Thank you, Thomas. You may if you wish. I give you permission."

"May what?" Remembering his resolve he pretended not to understand.

"Kiss me, of course. I'm told it's quite usual for a man to kiss a woman at a mabsant. Is that not so?"

"Yes, it is. Thank you for giving me permission." But he made no move. She waited expectantly.

"I daren't," he said at last.

"Daren't? Why not?" The eyes flashed. "Am I not attractive enough for you?"

"Attractive! You're the most beautiful woman I've ever seen. I thought that on the beach this afternoon."

"Yet still you hesitate. Is it because you think I am too young for you?"

"No, it's not that."

"Then surely it's not because you think me above you in any way—because if you do that's very foolish. You are far above me. I can't sing or compose music like you can, so don't let—"

"No, it's not that either."

She lowered her arms.

"What, then?"

He took a deep breath.

"I daren't kiss you because I know I would not be able to stop there. I would then want to make love to you, and if I did that—if you permitted me—I should fall in love also. And that's something that must never be allowed to happen."

For a few moments she just stared at him, then:

"Would falling in love with me be so dreadful?" she asked in a low voice.

"For me it would. It would be like glimpsing heaven and then having it torn away."

"Torn away? Good gracious! And do you think one kiss would lead to—to all that?"

"Not for you, perhaps. For you it would be one more conquest. For me it would be different—for I know I could never possess you."

"Oh, Thomas!" She was mischievous again now. "You can't be serious."

"I've never been so serious in my life."

"In that case you are a very honest man. Most men I know would require no second bidding."

"I know, but they're in a higher position in life than I am. They can entertain hopes of marrying you. I can't. That's why I dare not kiss you."

"Oh dear! So you would like to marry me then, Thomas. I am very flattered."

"I'm not flattering you. I'm just telling you that I never allow my mind to dwell on unobtainable things. I never have."

"I see. So that's why you think it unwise to kiss me, even at a mabsant?"

"Yes. I'm sorry. Please don't be offended."

"You haven't offended me, Thomas," she said softly. "I regard what you say as a compliment. But since you won't kiss me would you perhaps allow me to kiss you? It's nothing serious mind, so don't be alarmed. It's just a reward for singing so beautifully for me tonight."

Before he could reply she reached up and touched his cheeks with hands so cool they seemed to burn him. Then she drew his head down and kissed him lightly on the mouth.

"There, Thomas! You have your reward. Come now. We must return or your admirers will begin to wonder what I've done with their favourite singer."

She laughed, took his hand and pulled him along the path towards the Town Hall, now resounding to the sounds of a noisy quadrille. Suddenly he felt light-headed and happy, all thoughts of caution abandoned.

CHAPTER 3

ELIZABETH GENTLY OPENED the kitchen door and smiled at the sight of Janet dozing in the rocking chair, making occasional burbling noises with her lips. She wondered for a moment whether to tip-toe up to bed but the door creaked and Janet woke with a start. She stared confusedly about the room then caught sight of Elizabeth.

"So there you are! You're late."

"I told you not to wait up for me," scolded Elizabeth. "I had a key."

"I know but I couldn't go to bed knowing you were out on them moors."

"I was quite safe. I was escorted all the way home."

"Oh!" Janet woke up properly. "Who by?"

"Thomas Evans."

"Thomas Evans, the harpist from Newton! Well, he's got a long walk home tonight, I must say. Did you enjoy yourself?"

"Very much. I had a lovely time—I danced nearly every dance. It was much better than those old balls I went to in London."

"Who did you dance with altogether?"

"With Thomas mostly. Oh, and Janet! He sang two songs specially for me, one of them a completely new one, not heard around here before. He has a beautiful voice—the best I've ever heard. I could have listened to him all night."

Janet's rheumy eyes narrowed.

"Two songs specially for you, eh! Well, I must say you and Thomas Evans seem to have had a good time between you."

"Oh, we did! He's such a good dancer, too—and one of the nicest men I've met. I'm going to help him with some songs he's written—with the words, that is of course, not the music."

"Are you now? I don't know what your father'll have to say about that."

"I won't tell him. Anyway, what could he say? I'm nineteen now, not a child any more, so I shall do as I wish. Don't you tell him, though, Janet. I don't want him to know."

"He won't hear from my lips, but somebody'll let on about you, mark my words. Was Mark Edwards there?"

"Yes, I did catch a glimpse of him."

"Then he'll tell your father, that's for certain."

"Oh, what odds? Father can't stop me going and I shall again if I wish. Anyway, don't spoil such a lovely evening, Janet. I feel so happy at the moment. Here I am, back in Sker and just had one of the most enjoyable evenings of my life. But it's been a long day and I'm tired now so I shall go to bed. Don't wake me too early in the morning."

She went towards the door but as she reached it Janet called out.

"Elizabeth! I'd like to talk to you for a moment, please."

Elizabeth turned.

"Yes, Janet."

Janet pursed her lips, obviously having difficulty framing her words.

"You're a beautiful woman now. You know that, don't you?"

"Am I?" Elizabeth smiled. "That's very kind of you, Janet."

"I'm not being kind. You know you are. And it's beauty like yours that will give you power over men one day—great power if you use it aright. You may not realise it now but you will before long."

"Does it. I didn't think I was all that beautiful."

"Well, you are, and it's no secret that your father was hoping you'd use your looks to get a good husband. That's why he sent you and Mary away to London."

"I know, but it's rich husbands father's after. He wants some of the money for himself."

"Well, you can't blame him for that. He wants you both to do well for yourselves, so don't be too hard on him. He and me don't always see eye to eye, but I know what he's aiming at there. He can see sand encroaching everywhere on the fields and some of the buildings have been ruined by the wind. He don't want to lose Sker Manor."

"And neither do I. But Mary can make a good marriage for him. She's different from me. She likes wealth and position. I tell you this now, Janet: I would never marry anybody except for love, it doesn't matter what father says."

Janet sighed.

"It's possible to have both, Elizabeth. I'm only trying to help you. I promised your mother I'd do that before she died. Your father's already angry because you've come back from London alone—"

"Well, let him. I can't help it if I didn't meet anybody I liked, can I?"

"No, but don't cross him these days. He's got a terrible temper—fel yr hen diawl. And I must tell you this, too: there's been a man around here seeing him about you. I think he's been asking for your hand in marriage."

"Who's that?" asked Elizabeth quickly.

"Mr. Kirkhouse of Neath."

"Oh, him! He bores me to distraction. All he talks about is coal mines. And last year at the Tythegston ball he trod on my feet so much I had corns for days. He'd be the last man I'd want to marry."

"But he's serious about you, I think. I heard your father tell him he'd speak to you when he got back."

"Then let him. I shan't marry Mr. Kirkhouse come what may."

"Well, there's another thing, Elizabeth—and please take this kindly. I know Thomas Evans very well. A nicer man you won't find. I wouldn't like to see him hurt in any way."

Elizabeth's eyes widened in surprise.

"And neither would I. Who's going to hurt him?"

"You might, Elizabeth, if you're not careful. I'd hate for Thomas Evans to have expectations that couldn't be realised, and when a man dances with a girl all night and then sings songs for her there's reason to think he's interested in her. And if he believes there's a chance of marrying that girl and then finds his hopes dashed it'll go hard with him. I hope you haven't encouraged him with expectations in any way."

"Of course I haven't. I wouldn't hurt Thomas for worlds either. Like you I have too much respect for him."

"Well, from what I've just heard you've both been pretty thick tonight—and he brought you back home, didn't he? And now you're going to see him again. What am I to think of that and what will the people around here say? It don't take much to make tongues wag, I can tell you."

"Well, they can wag as much as they like. I enjoy Thomas's company, that's all—and anyway, he's happy as he is: a confirmed bachelor."

"A confirmed bachelor with aspirations, perhaps. When you see him next make your position plain to him, Elizabeth; your father will never allow you to marry anybody who's poor."

"Thomas isn't poor. He's not rich, I know, but with his work and music he makes a good living. Anyway, why all this talk of marriage? You're as bad as the village gossips, Janet. A few hours spent with a man and you start getting silly ideas."

"It's not silly ideas. I want to advise you, that's all. I've seen a lot with these old eyes. I think it would be wiser if you didn't see Thomas Evans again."

Elizabeth tried not to get angry.

"Now you're going too far, Janet. I shall see Thomas whenever I like. I've promised to help him with his songs and that I shall do. And I want you to know this too: if ever I should fall in love, and whenever that is, I would marry a man whether he was rich or poor—that is if he asked me, of course, and was also in love with me. Neither you nor my father would stop me. I've seen what unhappiness comes of marriages of convenience and I want none of them."

Janet shook her head, acknowledging defeat.

"Then I won't interfere any more, merch fach. I'll pray for your happiness, that's all, and trust that God will guide you."

"Thank you, Janet. If you do that then I'm sure all will be well. Now don't fuss any more. I promise you this: I'll never do anything to hurt Thomas or make you ashamed of me. Does that make you feel happier?"

Janet nodded dubiously. Elizabeth went to the door and lifted the latch.

"And now I really must go to bed. I can hardly keep my eyes open. Don't forget, Janet, don't call me until ten at the earliest."

She went upstairs, leaving Janet rocking furiously in the chair, deep in uneasy thought.

CHAPTER 4

WEARING A finely-tailored black riding habit and a small, plumed hat that accentuated the colour of her hair, Elizabeth cantered her favourite stallion down Moor Lane towards Nottage. As she neared the outskirts of the village several farm workers stopped work in the fields to stare at her, the women curtseying and the men touching their foreheads. Elizabeth smiled at them, pleased at the impression she was making, for she knew she looked her best in hunting costume.

At Nottage she turned off towards Newton and held the stallion down to a walk, for she did not wish to perspire before reaching her destination. Once in the village she made straight for the church and without difficulty found her objective: Thomas Evans's carpenter's shop. Dismounting, she drew the reins through an iron rung in the wall, gave a small, gaping boy a penny to look after the horse and knocked at the half open split-level door. Hearing no answer she pushed the door wider and went in. Thomas was at a bench, sawing a piece of wood. For a moment he did not see her, but when he did his mouth opened in surprise.

"Good morning, Thomas," said Elizabeth brightly. "I hope I haven't surprised you coming so early, but I wanted to see the songs as soon as possible. I hope you don't mind."

Recovering quickly Thomas drew the saw out of the wood and placed it on the bench.

"It is a surprise, Elizabeth, but a very pleasant one."

"You didn't think I was serious, did you? Well, I am. I promised to help you with the words, and so I shall. Can I have them now?"

Thomas went to a cupboard, rummaged around in a drawer and took out a roll of vellum.

"They're only rough drafts as I told you—a translation from the Welsh, but the metre is in time with the music, so any alterations must have the same number of syllables."

"Oh, I probably won't have to make any changes. If the words are as good as your music there'll be nothing to do."

"I don't know about that for only the Welsh words are mine. A friend translated them for me but I'm still not satisfied that they rhyme well. Anyway, have a good look at them and let me know what you think."

Elizabeth took the sheets and glanced at them.

"For what it's worth, Thomas, I shall. Give me just a day or two."

"Spend as long as you like over them. I'd rather they were correct."

"Oh, I'll have read them by tomorrow. Then another day formulating my ideas—if I have any that is—and I'll be able to tell you what I think. Oh, Thomas! I find it very exciting trying to help you. I've never done anything like this before. I feel as though I'm helping to create something. All I hope is what I suggest won't sound too naive."

"What you say won't sound naive, I'm sure of that."

"Don't be too sure." She undid the top button of her jacket and carefully placed the vellum inside. Suddenly she sniffed the air. "Oh, what a lovely smell. I noticed it when I came in. It's so—so fresh and likeable. Is it the wood?"

"The wood and the shavings. The glue, too, perhaps. Many people like the smell of glue."

She walked over to the bench and picked up a strange-looking tool.

"What's this?"

"A saw."

"A saw! I've never seen one like that before. It looks more like a harp to me."

"It's used for fine cutting—for delicate work."

"I see. And this?"

"That's a marker gauge. I can draw straight lines on the wood with that then I know where to cut."

She nodded and stooped over the bench.

"And this?"

"A love spoon. The start of it, that is. I only began it this morning."

"A love spoon, eh! May I enquire who it's for?"

"A lady."

"Do I know her?"

"It's possible."

"Then I wonder who she is. Can you tell me her name?"

"Not at the moment. I'm bound to secrecy."

"Oh, what a pity! Will you be able to tell me one day—when it's completed?"

"Perhaps."

She smiled mischievously at him.

"Then I must rest content until I know the identity of this fortunate lady." Suddenly she saw a small coffin lying on two trestles in the corner. "Oh dear! Then a child has died. You were telling me about that. Who is it?"

"Sian Roberts, the blacksmith's daughter. She died two days ago of the measles. She was only six."

"Poor little thing. It's such a tiny coffin. Isn't it a tragedy to bring a child into the world and then see it die so young, with hardly any experience of life?"

"Yes, a tragedy indeed."

She leaned forward, examining the coffin.

"I have heard, Thomas, that a woman's sure she's in love with a man when she knows she wants his child. Do you believe that to be true?"

"I believe so. It works the other way round, too, I think. When a man knows he wants a woman to bear his child it's fairly certain that he loves her. At least, that's what I've been told."

"Then it must be true." She looked thoughtfully at him for a moment, opened her mouth as though she was about to say something further, then changed her mind. Instead she patted the top of the vellum and sighed. "I do wish I could stay and talk to you about this, but I must go. There's some shopping I must do and then I have to return to Sker to meet my father. He's coming back from Neath today and I must be there when he arrives or he'll be angry. When shall I see you again to discuss the songs?"

"Any time you like. Perhaps the evening would be best when I've finished my work. I'll come up to Sker if you like."

"Oh, would you? But I'm afraid I can't ask you into the house. My father hasn't met you yet—and he's not too sociable these days."

"He has met me but I don't think he approves of me, so it's better that I don't call on you. Perhaps we could meet somewhere."

"There aren't many people my father does approve of, so don't worry about that. Do you know where Pwll Dafan is? If we could meet there it would be quiet and we wouldn't be disturbed."

"Yes, I know Pwll Dafan. When would you like me to come?"

"Say tomorrow night at about seven. I'll have everything ready by then."

"Seven it is, then. I'll be there."

She walked over to the door then turned to face him.

"I did enjoy last night, Thomas. Thank you for singing for me."

"It was a pleasure."

"I must tell you one thing before I go. It's been on my mind ever since last night. When I arrived home Janet, our housekeeper, was waiting up for me, and when I told her that we had danced together most of the night and that you'd brought me home—and that I was seeing you again—she said something about being afraid I was trying to lead you astray, or words to that effect. You didn't think that, did you, Thomas? I had to reassure her that there was nothing more than friendship between us."

"You were right to say that," he said uneasily.

"I didn't tell her that I had kissed you."

"It's better that you didn't."

"And neither did I mention what you'd said about—about your fear of becoming involved with me in case it led to—to something more."

"I spoke the truth when I said that."

"I know. Janet and I had quite a heated argument. It ended with my telling her that I'd never marry a man for wealth—only for love, and that I was old enough to make up my own mind."

Thomas opened his mouth to reply but she gave him no chance.

"And do you know, Thomas, she had to admit that I was right. So you see, you are in good hands as I told you. I promised Janet that I would never do anything to hurt you. So you need have no qualms about meeting me—tomorrow or any other time."

"I never had any."

"Good! Then I shall see you tomorrow night."

She smiled and went outside. Thomas went with her and helped her mount. Watched by a small group of curious villagers she waved and rode off down the cobbled street. Thomas nodded at the spectators as though Elizabeth's visit was a daily occurrence, and he had just completed a business transaction with her, then returned to the workshop. He picked up the love spoon, stared at it for a moment, then took up a knife and began carving. It was the most intricate love spoon he had ever devised.

CHAPTER 5

After purchasing needles and cotton at the village shop Elizabeth rode quickly back to Sker across the moors, avoiding the lanes in case carts and flocks of sheep impeded her progress, for she wanted to be home before her father arrived. But as she approached the house her heart sank, for Dafydd was already leading his roan into the stables and there was a strange carriage and pair outside the front door. She dismounted, threw the reins to Dafydd and went into the kitchen. Janet was piling plates on the table and darting occasionally to the fireplace. She gave Elizabeth an anxious look.

"There's glad I am you've come. Your father's back with Mr. Kirkhouse and some people from Neath. They're staying for the midday meal."

Elizabeth threw her crop on a chair.

"Oh dear! I did so want to be back when he arrived. Was he angry not to find me here?"

"He didn't seem pleased. I told him you'd gone shopping. He's still annoyed about London, I think. I heard him tell Mr. Savours that. You'd better go up and see them—they're in the banqueting room."

"Oh, well! I suppose I'd better get it over with."

She went upstairs and gingerly pushed open the door of the banqueting room. She could see her father, glass in hand, standing near the fireplace talking to his three guests. She took a deep breath and went in.

"Ah, Elizabeth!" Isaac sounded surprisingly genial. "At last I see you. Where've you been?"

"Shopping, father. It was also a good excuse to get some fresh air after London."

"Ah, yes, London! We'll speak about that later. Come, you remember Mr. and Mrs. Savours, of course, and Mr. Kirkhouse you know very well."

Both men bowed and Kirkhouse held out his hand. He was a tall, sandy-haired, spare-framed man of about thirty, soberly dressed in black. In a strong, north-country accent he said:

"How are you, Elizabeth? It's some time since I saw you last."

"And even longer for me," said Mrs. Savours, stout, bleached and tightly-corseted. "How long is it now? It must be all of two years. You've grown into quite a woman in that time—a good-looking woman, too, if I may say so."

"More than good-looking," said her husband admiringly. "Handsome is a better word. Congratulations, Isaac. I didn't know you had it in you to produce such a beauty."

"Oh!" said Isaac, staring narrow-eyed at Elizabeth over his glass, "she takes after her mother in that respect."

"I can see that," replied Savours, "but she's taller and more—more strapping. I hear you've been to London, Elizabeth. Did you like it there?"

"Apparently not," said Isaac drily. "She came home and left her sister there."

"Didn't enjoy London!" exclaimed Mrs. Savours. "Why ever not?"

"It was dirty," replied Elizabeth wearily. "And there were too many people there for my liking."

"Oh, well," said Savours, "I suppose one can understand that. After all, if you're country-bred towns are stuffy places. After the moors and sea it must have been a bit claustrophobic for you, eh, Elizabeth?" He winked and prodded her with an elbow.

"Yes", said Elizabeth gratefully, "it was."

Kirkhouse, who was still in awe of Elizabeth, gave a nervous laugh.

"Then London's loss is Kenfig's gain. I am so glad to see you home again, Elizabeth."

Elizabeth gave him a frigid stare.

"You left Mary quite well, I take it," he went on, undeterred. "I mean to say, she hasn't returned with you, has she? So perhaps—"

"Mary knows which side her bread is buttered," interjected Isaac. "She's got more sense than Elizabeth here. This one's wilful."

"Oh, come, sir!" said Kirkhouse. "Elizabeth has a great deal of common sense, too. I know that. Surely—"

"I'm glad you think so," said Isaac. "But be warned. If you see much of her from now on you'll need to be on the firm side. She needs breaking in like a good mare."

"Father!" Elizabeth stamped her foot. "Please don't compare me with a horse."

"There!" said Isaac, winking. "What did I tell you? Mettlesome as ever. You'll have to look out, Kirkhouse, I warn you, if you come here often. But she's got her points, I grant you."

Kirkhouse nodded several times, a look of euphoria on his face.

"Indeed, I have always thought so. Your father has given me permission to call on you, Elizabeth. You have no objection, I trust."

Elizabeth opened her mouth to reply but Isaac gave her no chance. "She won't object, I promise you that. You can talk to her later about it. Now you must excuse us for a moment. Elizabeth and I must have a little chat about a certain matter, and then she's got to change and make herself presentable. Make yourselves at home and help yourselves to the sack. There's plenty of it. I'll be back presently."

He took Elizabeth by the arm and propelled her gently but firmly from the room. He kept behind her all the way up the stairs and followed her into her bedroom. Knowing what was coming Elizabeth went to the window and stared petulantly out of it. Isaac took a deep breath, trying to control his temper.

"Well! I want to know why you came back from London so soon."

"I told you in my letter," said Elizabeth, still facing the window. "I didn't care for it there."

"You know why I sent you in the first place, don't you? I was hoping you'd have met some important and influential people there. Your sister is happy enough. She's making the most of it. Why can't you be as amenable as she is?"

"My sister's a different person from me."

Isaac's face reddened.

"I don't understand you, Elizabeth. You know the difficulties, I'm in, don't you? Turn round and answer me."

Elizabeth turned.

"I know them very well, father. But it's no good relying on me. I've told you before, I can't stand London and wish only to remain here."

"Then have a care or there won't be a home for you to return to one day. That riding habit you're wearing is just a pretence—it hasn't been paid for yet. Neither has the horse you've been gallivanting about on. So far I've kept ahead of my creditors and not many know of my predicament. I was hoping that by now you'd have understood. But it seems you cannot or will not."

"Father! I'd do all in my power to help you. I don't want us to be impoverished either. But I cannot possibly marry a man for whom I have no regard—especially somebody I might have met in London. We've spoken about this before and I've made my feelings plain to you."

"Dammit, girl! It's not just myself I'm thinking of—can't I get you to see that? It's you and Mary I'm concerned about. If I do become poor not many men—men of standing, that is—would want either of you. As it is—as things appear at the moment—you are both still very eligible young women. Surely it's not unreasonable to—to want to kill two birds with one stone, so to speak. You could both do very well for yourselves, particularly you, Elizabeth, with your looks. Mary can attract men, too, of course, but not like you. I've seen how you get on at the balls and banquets we've been to. Why, only last year at Nottage Court you were the centre of attraction. Kirkhouse was quite put out because he couldn't get near you—"

"And now you've given him permission to call on me knowing how much I dislike him."

"You don't give him a chance, girl. The fellow's mad gone on you. Any fool can see that, so why shouldn't I give him permission? Anyway, to my way of thinking this is your last chance and I don't want you being silly or rude to him. Remember this: he's rich and could provide for you in a way few other men around here could. Don't turn him down out of hand. Let him see you for a while and then perhaps you'll get to like him. Do as I say and think it over. You'll see that what I'm saying makes sense."

Elizabeth unpinned her hat and threw it on a chair.

"I see no sense in marrying without love, and Mr. Kirkhouse is a man I could never love—not in a hundred years."

"Why not, for God's sake? He's kind and well-liked, ain't he? He's quiet, I grant you, and in your presence he's always a bit tongue-tied. But that's because he's keen on you. If you ask me he's got enough love for the both of you. Give him a chance, I say. You're not being fair to the man."

"Oh, father! Why the hurry? Can't you wait a little longer? Then, perhaps, one day, someone will come along—"

"One day! By Christmas I'll be in the poor house if things don't get better. No, Elizabeth, I tell you now: you must make the effort to like Kirkhouse. I grant you love won't come immediately but he's got a fine house in Briton Ferry and you'll have a carriage and pair in no time. Dresses galore, too, and a horse of your own like here—"

"And that's all you really think about, isn't it? Wordly possessions."

"Well, dammit!—they count for a great deal, don't they? You can't do without 'em, say what you like."

"I could. Have you no idea of what you're asking me to do? Don't you realise what misery marriage without affection can be? At best it's an existence; at worst it's a—a hell on earth, and it goes on for a lifetime. Take Aunt Mary in London. Have you ever seen such relief when Uncle Jack died? She nearly wept for joy—it was the end of twenty years of misery for her. She looked younger overnight. Is that what you want of me?"

"We-ell," he said grudgingly, "I grant you that marriage wasn't a success. But you don't necessarily have to love a man before you marry him. That comes later, quite often."

"How often? I've never seen it."

"Well, you can't live in poverty either. Believe me, poverty ruins more marriages than riches."

"Do you have to have either? Most people seem to live quite happily without existing in either extreme."

Isaac shook his head in exasperation.

"You can argue the hind leg off a donkey, Elizabeth. You put me in mind of your mother there. Once you've got something in your head nothing will get it out. But I tell you this, and I'm warning you: don't go against me over Kirkhouse. I've given him permission to call on you and by damn, you're going to see him, come hell or high water. You've ruined your chances in London through sheer obstinacy—after me spending money I could ill afford on you—but you're not going to turn down a chance like this. Get changed now and be back downstairs within half an hour. If you're not there by then, by damn, I'll come and fetch you myself."

He went over to the door then turned.

"And if you're not nice and polite to Kirkhouse, I'll lock you in your room for the rest of the week—see if I don't. If you're going to act like a child I'll damn well treat you like one. You're not too old for that yet. So remember what I've said."

He went out and slammed the door behind him. Elizabeth undid her jacket and threw it on the bed. Then she let her skirt fall and stamped on it.

CHAPTER 6

By seven o'clock the tide was full in, making quiet lapping sounds in the crevices and runnels of Pwll Dafan. From her cove just above the creek Elizabeth watched the gentle swell rocking the fronds of seaweed to and fro and thought about the last few days. Her joy at returning home and attending the mabsant had been suddenly eclipsed by her father's intransigence. She had always known that he wanted her to marry well but had not thought deeply about it, assuming that one day a suitor would appear who was acceptable to both of them. But that was before she had met Thomas Evans, and so the future was filled with foreboding. She thought about Thomas constantly now. If only he had been of nobler birth or even a yeoman farmer all would be well, but her father would never consent to her marrying him, assuming of course that Thomas ever asked her. She was certain of only one thing: she would never marry Mr. Kirkhouse. That was as certain as the sun now descending over Hartland Point, but it would mean a constant and wearing battle of attrition with her father. She sighed and looked around the cove. Life was uncomplicated when her only passion had been collecting shells from the beach.

She glanced at the vellum lying in her lap. She had studied the songs carefully in the privacy of her room and had come to the conclusion that only a few alterations need be made; but in order not to appear presumptuous she had written her suggestions on scraps of paper and pinned them to the parchment. Then, if Thomas disagreed, they could easily be removed. She thought that what she had done was an improvement on the original words, but she would not take offence if her efforts were rejected; and in any case she had enjoyed the task. She placed the sheets on the sand beside her and settled back more comfortably against the rocky ledge to await Thomas's arrival.

After a few minutes she heard the scrunch of feet on the shingle and looked up to see him approaching. His eyes lit up when he saw her.

"Good evening, Elizabeth. I didn't expect you to be here so soon. I thought I was in good time."

"You are," said Elizabeth, "but I had nothing else to do so I thought I'd come here and wait for you. I've been going over the alterations I've made. I do hope you approve of them."

He sat down beside her.

"Oh, I'm sure I will. Let me see."

He took the vellum and read carefully. Elizabeth watched him anxiously and at last he nodded.

"Yes. I like the word 'ache' instead of 'pain'. 'Ache of a broken heart' sounds better than 'pain of a broken heart'. Also 'clinging to' sounds nicer than 'tenacious'. Yes, Indeed, I prefer those. And I see you've changed a Welsh word, too! You've put 'caredig' instead of 'serchog'.

"Yes. I thought 'caredig' sounded better than 'serchog'—in that context, anyway."

"Yes, it does—I agree with you. I didn't know you spoke Welsh, Elizabeth."

"Oh, just a little. My mother taught me some and Janet often speaks to me in Welsh. I wish I were better at it."

"You must be quite good to have altered 'serchog' to 'caredig'. I also like 'wretchedness' in the last verse. It's more effective than 'unhappiness'. Yes, I like the changes very much."

Elizabeth felt a glow of satisfaction steal over her.

"The first song was quite easy, I thought. I could see what should be done immediately. But I'm not sure of the second. I made only one alteration there."

"Yes, so I see: 'lucid' instead of 'clear'. I think I prefer 'lucid', come to think of it and they're both words of two syllables. It sounds better when you're trying to describe a person's thoughts. Indeed, you've put the finishing touches to them, I believe."

"Oh, do you really think so?" Elizabeth tried not to sound smug. "I'm so glad you're pleased. I did enjoy trying to help you. Do you always write your songs in Welsh first?"

"Always. It's my first tongue. But I must have translations ready for singing to English-speaking audiences. Then I sing one verse in Welsh and one in English to be polite. It would be rude to do otherwise. Mind you, I don't decry English—it's such a rich language, the language of Shakespeare."

"Which do you prefer—English or Welsh? To sing in, I mean."

"Oh, Welsh, of course. It's much more musical than English. English is very strong—majestic, I would say; but give me Welsh for singing any time—love songs and hymns especially."

Elizabeth cupped her hands behind her head and wriggled down so that she was lying more comfortably on the sand.

"Isn't it a pity more Welsh isn't spoken around here? Every day I hear more and more English, especially in the market places."

"Well, that's to be expected. You must remember that for centuries Kenfig was a Norman stronghold, and Newton was a Norman village. That's why English is so strong in these parts."

"In that case why don't we speak French? That's what the Normans spoke, isn't it?"

"Ah! That shows the power of English, doesn't it? It's not often the language of a defeated race gets the better of the language of the conqueror, but that's what happened in this case. That's why they speak English in England today and not French. Mind you, it shows the power of Welsh, too—so far it's held its own against both English and French. But if I'm to be honest with you I like English as well as Welsh. Each has its own strength. I like English for drama and Welsh for singing. It's my wish that one day every Welshman will speak both languages equally well. Don't you agree?"

Elizabeth did not reply immediately for she had been studying Thomas as he spoke his animated words. At last she found her voice.

"Yes, I agree. When shall I hear you sing the songs?"

"Oh, when I've perfected them—just as you've perfected the words. I think I'm like an artist I met once who wouldn't let anybody see his paintings until he'd finished them. It's like a mother who won't show her baby to anyone until it's properly dressed."

"Then I must be patient and wait. There speaks the true artist himself—always striving for perfection."

"Well, I want these songs to be right, especially as you've helped me. Give me a week or so and then I'll let you hear them."

"Very well." Elizabeth wriggled again until she was almost lying full length on the sand. She stared up at the sky. "Oh, isn't it a lovely evening? I can't see a single cloud."

Thomas glanced up.

"It is, indeed. We've had such good weather recently that even the farmers aren't grumbling."

"Then that is indeed a miracle. Thomas! I've been thinking about you. Janet told me you'd not married because you had a widowed mother and several brothers and sisters to look after. You didn't tell me that."

"Only because it's no longer true. I did look after them once but all my brothers and sisters have grown up or married now. I told you the real reason—I've never met the woman I wanted to marry."

"And what sort of woman would you like to marry?"

"Well, I've often thought about it, I suppose. I'd like her to be kind and gentle, of course. Above all, I think, I'd want her to take an interest in my work—music, that is—to help me as you've done tonight. I'd also like her to enjoy good books, if that's possible, so that we could discuss them; and I know

I'd want her to be good-looking, for I must be honest: every man likes to have an attractive wife. I—I suppose it's because I've wanted all these things that I've never found her. So now I must be content with my music—she's a mistress, really, a very demanding one."

"And you've never met such a woman?"

"Well, I have, if I must be truthful."

"Where did you meet her?"

"Not far from here. I don't think about her, though, for I know she's unobtainable."

"Another unobtainable woman! You are unfortunate, Thomas. You seem to meet many unobtainable women. You said I was unobtainable, too."

"Yes. Most unfortunate, isn't it?"

She turned her head and smiled at him.

"Thomas, when I kissed you on the night of the mabsant you didn't think I was forward, did you?"

"No, of course not."

"It was a form of thanks for such a lovely evening—for singing to me."

"Yes, I know. It was a lovely evening for me, too, and I was pleased to sing for you."

"I've also been thinking about what you said—the reason you gave for not wanting to kiss me. You were serious when you said that, weren't you?"

"Yes, indeed I was."

"If I remember correctly you said you didn't want to kiss me because you were afraid of falling in love with me—because I was unobtainable also. That's what you said, wasn't it?"

"Yes."

"Then am I the second unobtainable woman you've met recently?"

He looked away from her suddenly.

"No, there's only one, really."

"Who is she?"

"I can't tell you."

"A secret, is it? Like the lady who will receive the love spoon?"

"Yes."

"Is it me?"

"Yes." He faced her again. "I must admit it."

"But you only met me two days ago, Thomas. Surely you don't mean that in such a short time you'd like to fall in love with me—if you allowed yourself to, that is."

"I can't help how I feel," he said dully. "All I know is that what I'd like and what I can have are two different things."

"But why, Thomas? Why would you like to fall in love with me?"

"I thought you'd know that by now. You're all the things I've just mentioned—you're beautiful and kind, and you love music. You're everything I desire in a woman. It's just my bad luck that I've met you late in life and that you're Elizabeth Williams of Sker Manor—and I'm Thomas Evans, the village carpenter."

"What's wrong with being a carpenter? It's a very highly respected calling. Jesus was a carpenter."

"It may be highly respected among ordinary people, but not to the gentry. And I know full well that one day you'll have to marry into that gentry. That's why I've not allowed myself to think about you—or kiss you, as I've told you."

"And yet you've made a love spoon. Is it for me?"

"Yes. But I wouldn't have given it to you."

"Why not? Isn't that what love spoons are for? To show someone that you love them?"

He waved a hand desperately.

"It was just a silly notion—very silly indeed."

"It's not silly at all. Then tell me, Thomas, if I'd been a village girl living in Newton, would you have courted me?"

"Yes, of course, if I could have got near to you in the press of other suitors."

"How long have you been thinking like this about me?"

"Ever since I met you on the beach, I think. You looked so beautiful and you showed such interest in my music—and I felt the same way at the mabsant. Indeed, if the truth were to be told I think I even fell in love with you when you were just a little girl all those years ago at the enquiry. You were delightful then—quite adorable, and I remember wondering what you'd be like when you grew up. Now I know, and you haven't left my thoughts since the night of the mabsant, although I tried to stop myself. I've told myself not to be foolish, for I'm more realist than romantic in spite of being a musician. That's why I didn't kiss you then. I didn't want to start anything that would lead to—to—"

"You're very sure you can't possess me, Thomas," she said softly. "Then what would you say if I told you I'd like you to fall in love with me? What would you say to that?"

He stared at her as though he had not heard correctly.

"I'd say the same thing. I wouldn't allow myself to even begin."

"Then what if I went further and told you that I would like to fall in love with you?" She emphasised the words 'I' and 'you'. "Would you have an answer to that?"

He looked so confused she laughed, but almost immediately reached up and touched his cheek.

"Please listen, Thomas. I must be honest with you, just as you've been with me. You're right in thinking I may have to marry into gentry. My father has told me so. But I do not love the man he has chosen for me. Rather than do that I would run away. I could get work, as a governess, perhaps, or even as a seamstress—I'm quite good at sewing—but I'll do anything not to marry this man. My father can threaten all he likes."

"Is he threatening you?"

"Indeed he is."

"And there's no other way out—except by running away?"

"None that I can see. My father is adamant about it."

"I'm sorry. You must be very unhappy."

"Of course, there is another alternative."

"What's that?"

"If you could allow yourself to fall in love with me—and if I fell in love with you—we could marry, couldn't we? Would you like to marry me, Thomas?"

He stared at her.

"I feel the same way as you, Thomas," she went on quickly. "It's only a short time since we met but from the moment I saw you sitting alone on the beach singing to yourself I knew I could fall in love with you. I dreamed about you that very night, and it may be that fate meant us to meet like that. But please don't think I'm telling you this because I'm trying to avoid a marriage I don't want. I just know deep down inside me that I could be happy with you—very happy, for the rest of my life—and I felt even surer at the mabsant. And if you think the same about me I don't see why we shouldn't marry. Do you? Answer me truly."

He nodded then slid down a little so that he was half lying on the sand beside her.

"I would dearly like to marry you," he said quietly. "But we must think about it for a moment. Your father would prevent it somehow. He's too influential and knows all the parsons for miles around. He'd stop us before we could even start. It would mean going away."

"And that would mean you leaving Newton and your family. You wouldn't like that, would you."

"Oh, I wouldn't worry about that as long as I could be with you; but there are other things to think of as well. I would have to tell my family. I couldn't just disappear without letting them know. Then I must get my tools together, for I must work to support you, although my music will make sure we don't starve."

Suddenly her eyes became moist.

"Oh, Thomas! Do you really think we could go away together? You won't regret it, I promise you. I'll make you the best wife in the world. I don't require riches, only enough to live on. We can find somewhere to live and you can work and I'll look after you. I'll do everything to please you. I give you my word on that."

For the first time he smiled.

"I know that, Elizabeth, but you'll please me by just being with me. Perhaps we could go to England, or to Carmarthen, where my family came from—we could find a cottage somewhere in the country and—"

"Oh, yes! I'd love that. Any old place will do and I'll turn it into a real home for us—you'll see."

Slowly, hesitantly, he put his arms around her, but he was still unsure of himself.

"Ever since the mabsant I—I've dreamed of being able to do this. It seems like a dream to me now. Please tell me I'm not dreaming, Elizabeth. Tell me that it really is you—and that you really do love me—and won't go back on your word about marrying me."

Elizabeth laughed and cried at the same time.

"Yes, Thomas, it really is me and I really do love you—and I won't go back on my word about marrying you."

"Then I will kiss you now, if I may, and after that there will be no going back—not for me, anyway."

"And not for me, either. From now on we will be together."

Thomas kissed her, clumsily at first then with greater passion. Elizabeth responded hungrily and the kiss became a long-drawn-out affair, so neither saw a figure standing on a hummock just above the cove. It was Mark Edwards, grinning hugely. He watched the couple for a moment then, still grinning, walked in the direction of Sker House.

CHAPTER 7

It was nearly dark when Elizabeth arrived home. She made straight for her room but as she passed the door of the banqueting hall she saw a light inside and halted. Through the jamb she could see her father standing by the fireplace, a scowl on his face. She gathered up her dress and tip-toed past but before she had gone two paces she heard his voice.

"Elizabeth! Come here."

She dropped her dress and went into the room.

"Yes, father. I didn't know you were here."

He stared at her, a nerve twitching in his cheek, sure indication that trouble was in store.

"Where've you been?"

"Out, father. Just walking."

"Just walking, eh! As far as the beach, I take it. Did you see anybody down there?"

"No. It was quite deserted."

"Deserted, was it? You're lying, girl. I know who you were with."

"Do you, father?" Elizabeth tried to keep her voice steady.

"You were with that damned Thomas Evans, weren't you? It's no good you denying it. Had you arranged to meet him there?" His voice rose suddenly to a shout.

"Yes. I was helping him with some songs he's composed."

"Helping him with songs he's composed! How long has this been going on?"

"It's the first time."

"The first time since you went to the mabsant with him, I suppose. I've been told you were there as well. Well! Weren't you? Answer me."

"Yes."

"Going to a public function with a common fellow like Thomas Evans a—a mere carpenter! Is that the way I've brought you up to behave? Well! I'm waiting for an explanation."

She tried to make herself as tall as possible.

"I can go to a mabsant if I wish, surely, and Thomas Evans isn't a common fellow. He's well-read and well-mannered."

"Well-mannered enough to make love to you on a beach like a common whore. So this is what's going on behind my back! Well, I can tell you this now: it's going to stop, do you hear? No daughter of mine is going to act like that. Have you no shame, girl?"

"I've nothing to be ashamed of."

"Nothing to be ashamed of! Mark Edwards saw you out there—fornicating in the open for all to see. That's reason enough to be ashamed."

"We weren't fornicating. I love Thomas and he loves me. We would marry if you'd let us."

"Marry Thomas Evans!" Isaac's face went almost black. "Over my dead body! I've never heard anything so ludicrous in all my life—and this will put a stop to it. Do you know what this is? I received it today." He fumbled in a pocket and took out a letter. "This is from Thomas Kirkhouse. It outlines a proposal for a dowry for you—a very generous dowry. He's coming here on Friday to see you, to ask formally for your hand in marriage—formally, mark you, not creeping up underhandedly on the dunes. And d'you know what I'm going to tell him after what I've just heard? I'm going to tell him he can have it—that you'll marry him, come what may. Is that understood?"

"You're selling me, father, like one of your prize heifers."

"God-damn it, girl!" Isaac was roaring now. "I'm not selling you! Can't I get you to see sense? I'm doing my best for you, as any father would. In any case I can tell you this: whatever happens from now on you're not going to see Thomas Evans again. Not at any time. Ever! Is that plain enough for you?"

She gave him a scornful look and turned to go, but he seized her by the wrist, jerking her round.

"Oh, no, my girl! You don't go when I'm speaking to you. If you disobey me in this so much the worse for you. You're going to wed Kirkhouse come hail or sunshine. I'll see that you do if it's only to get you away from the clutches of that bloody carpenter."

She tried to wrest her arm away but his nails cut into her flesh.

"No, father," she managed. "You may be able to stop me seeing Thomas Evans but you'll never get me to marry Mr. Kirkhouse. I despise him."

"Oh, won't I? We'll see about that. Now understand this: from now on I forbid you to leave this house without my permission. Go to your room and stay there. Only when you begin to show common sense will you be allowed out. I've told you before and I tell you again, if you act like a child you'll be treated like one. No food will be allowed past your lips until you become reasonable. If I as much as see you downstairs or in the yard I'll lock you in properly and you won't even be allowed to go to the privy. No child of mine is going to make a fool of me in front of every Tom, Dick or Harry in the county. Go to your room now and stay there until I send for you—and by then, by God, you'd better be sensible."

He flung her arm away from him. Elizabeth remained where she was for a moment, as though she was about to argue further, but suddenly she turned and swept out of the hall. She kept up her composure until she reached her room but once inside she flung herself down on the bed and wept until nausea overcame her. For an hour she lay there, deep in the throes of misery, but just as she was about to reach for the chamber pot to relieve a bout of retching, an idea exploded in her mind with the force of a thunderbolt. She twisted herself round and stared at the ceiling. There was a way out and she had been a fool not to have thought of it before. She and Thomas had already half planned an elopement: now it must be brought forward. There should be no great difficulty in speeding things up, and if they could get away before Kirkhouse's arrival so much the better. Buoyed suddenly with renewed hope, she clambered off the bed, went to the bureau and took out her writing material.

But before she could dip the quill in the ink there was a knock at the door. Elizabeth thrust quill and paper out of sight and looked round fearfully, but it was only Janet carrying a tray covered with a napkin.

"I've brought this for you," Janet whispered. "I heard your father railing at you. He's no right to keep you without supper whatever you've done."

Elizabeth retrieved the quill and began writing.

"Thank you, Janet. He didn't see you, did he? I don't know what he'd do if he caught you trying to help me."

Janet's lower lip jutted out.

"No, he didn't see me, and if he do I'll give him a piece of my mind. He may think he can do as he likes with you but he can't with me. For shame on the man, treating his own daughter like that."

Elizabeth went on writing.

"Come what may, Janet, I'm not going to marry Mr. Kirkhouse. Put the tray down somewhere and come over here. I'm going to ask you to do something for me."

Janet placed the tray on the bedside table and went to stand by the bureau. For several minutes there was no sound except the scrape of quill on paper, then Elizabeth read what she had written and sealed the letter.

"Thomas Evans and I are going away together, Janet. Now don't look so shocked. It's all arranged only now we must act more quickly. This is a message asking him to fetch me tomorrow night. Do you know anybody reliable who can deliver it for me?"

Janet stared aghast at her.

"Oh, Duw, Elizabeth! Are you doing the right thing? I know you don't want to marry Mr. Kirkhouse but are you wise to—to—"

"Thomas and I love each other, Janet. We are quite certain about that. We shall be married and then father won't be able to do a thing about it. We had already arranged to go away in any case, and Thomas will start a business somewhere, and we'll be able to live together as man and wife. We will be very happy together."

Janet sank back against the bureau for support.

"Oh, Duw! You do fright me, talking like this. What about Mr. Kirkhouse? He'll be here on Friday."

"What about him? Do you want me to marry a man for whom I haven't the slightest affection?"

"No, of course not. You know that, but—"

"Well, then, Janet, you must help me. I'm not being unfair to Mr. Kirkhouse. I've never encouraged him in any way, so he's no right to expect my hand in marriage—and my father has no right to give it. Anyway, we shall be gone before he arrives."

"But are you quite sure about what you're doing? I mean that Thomas Evans loves you. You've only known him a few days it seems to me, and he's so much older than you—"

"I'm quite sure, Janet. I've never been surer of anything in my life before, and when two people love each other as much as we do the difference in our ages means nothing.

Janet's eyes became cloudy. She took a rag and blew her nose.

"Well then, if you're as certain as that I'll help you all I can, even if what I'm doing is wrong. I'll take the letter myself first thing in the morning."

"No, Janet! You mustn't go. If my father misses you he'll become suspicious. Surely there must be someone we can both trust."

Janet thought for a moment.

"Well, there's Iestyn Grabham, the cow-hand. I've looked after him ever since he's been here because he's got no mother—given him cakes and things like that. You've been kind to him, too, and he's too twp to realise what's going on. I could send him, I suppose."

Elizabeth handed her the letter.

"Then let Iestyn take it, only send him tonight without fail. I've asked Thomas to be here tomorrow at midnight. He knows where he can get a carriage. I shall give him a signal when it's safe, like this—"

She stood up, took the lamp and drew it three times across the window, an action that made Janet tremble.

"Oh, Iesu Grist! I'll pray for you, Elizabeth, but I must tell you now I never thought it would come to this. When you were a little girl I always thought you'd marry somebody who'd—who'd give you a proper church wedding, and now to think of you running away like this—"

"We'll have a church wedding, Janet, only not here."

"Well, if you say so, cariad, but it's a pity all the same. I just wish things could be done proper and above board, not like this."

"But if I'm happy that's all that matters, isn't it?" Elizabeth was impatient now. "And you should be happy for me, too. Haven't you always said that my happiness has been your main concern since mother died?"

"Yes, it always has been. You know that."

"Well, then, no more tears. I'm going to be very happy with Thomas for the rest of my life. If I wasn't sure of that I wouldn't go away with him. Go now, Janet, and see Iestyn. My whole future rests on that letter getting safely to Thomas tonight."

Janet slipped the letter under her shawl. Quickly she stooped and kissed Elizabeth.

"God be with you and take care of you tomorrow night. If anything should happen to you I don't know what I'd do."

She shuffled from the room, still blowing her nose. Elizabeth watched her go then ran to the wardrobe and flung open the door. Rapidly she took out her best dresses and placed them side by side on the bed.

CHAPTER 8

THOMAS EVANS tested the padlock on the door of his premises, looked up at the window of the room where his mother and youngest sister lay asleep, and breathed a sigh of relief. The fetching and loading of the carriage had disturbed no-one and they would find his note on the work-bench next morning. What they and the villagers would say when they knew he had eloped with Isaac Williams' younger daughter he could only contemplate, and there had been no time to explain things fully. He took out the watch he had bought the day before and saw that it was eleven o'clock. So far everything had gone smoothly and there was a half moon, with just enough light to see but not enough to make him conspicuous. He felt along the luggage deck, checking that the three boxes of tools, portmanteau and specially-made case containing his best harp were securely tied. Finally he touched the inner pocket of his new velvet jacket to make sure that the purse containing thirty gold sovereigns, his life savings, was still intact and climbed on the driving seat. Gently he flicked the reins and the horses moved off.

At first he was afraid of being challenged by the night watchman for the horses, although walking, made an inordinate amount of noise, the clatter of their hooves echoing back from the walls of the cottages; but he reached the outskirts of the village without mishap and allowed the animals to break into a trot until they reached Moor Lane. At St. David's well he reined them to a halt and lit one of the carriage lamps from his tinder box. By its light he scrutinised his watch again, nodded in approval and placed the lamp near his feet deep down in the driving well. His mouth felt dry and the muscles of his stomach tense.

After waiting ten minutes he moved off again, keeping the spirited pair to a slow walk. Soon he came to the driveway of Sker Manor where he dismounted to open the gates, wedging them back with stones so that nothing would impede a quick get-away. Mercifully neither horses nor carriage made much noise on the dirt track and even the creaking of the harnesses was drowned by the increasingly loud rumble of the sea. He reached the inner boundary wall, tied the horses to a gate post and walked forward a few yards so that he could see the front of the house, dark and intimidating against the purple of the sky. There was no light anywhere and still no sound except the grating of the under-tow. Satisfied, he returned to the carriage and retrieved the lamp. Holding it between his body and the house he kept close to the wall until he reached a point where he could see all the front windows; Elizabeth had told him in her letter from which one the signal would come, but he wanted to make sure. To ease his mounting excitement he leaned against the wall, the lamp ready at his feet.

* * * * *

Elizabeth dragged her fully-laden valise from its hiding place in the wardrobe and placed it ready near the door. She glanced quickly round to make sure she had forgotten nothing and nervously dropped a second hair brush into a small travelling bag. She flung a cloak over her shoulders, pressed the repeater of her fob-watch and went to the window. The faint, metallic pinging told her that it was midnight, so she drew back the curtain and peered across the silvery roofs of the out-buildings. By pressing her face hard against the panes she could just make out the far end of the boundary wall. With an unsteady hand she reached for the table lamp and drew it three times across the panes. She looked out again and at first could see nothing. Then she saw the answering flashes, faint but unmistakable, and her heart began to pound. She replaced the lamp on the table, went to the door and listened intently. Everything seemed to be quiet. She picked up the valise and made her way along the landing, testing each floor-board before putting her full weight on it. At the top of the stairs she paused again. Except for the faint ticking of the grandfather clock in the hall there was still no sound. Slowly and carefully she descended, counting each step to make sure she would not stumble at the bottom. She reached the hall and felt her way along the wall to the kitchen door. A few more paces and she would be out in the fresh air, running across the yard to Thomas.

But as she lifted the latch and eased back the door instinct told her that something was wrong; the kitchen did not have the unmistakable silence of an empty room. She paused, one foot over the threshold, unsure whether to go in.

Suddenly, from behind the settle a shadowy figure appeared. It came towards her and she saw that it was Mark

Edwards, holding up a hand from which a key was dangling. She stared at the key, petrified, the valise slipping from her grasp, then turned and ran. But he was too quick for her. Darting forward he seized her by the wrist.

"Sorry, miss, master's orders. I'm to lock you in your room."

She struggled with all her strength, but it was no use. She was dragged like a sack of corn back up the stairs and bundled into her room. She leaped forward to prevent the door being closed but the key grated in the lock before she could reach it. She pummelled at it with her fists and wrenched the door knob to and fro, but the heavy oak merely taunted her. Then, with a shock of fear, she remembered Thomas. Not knowing quite what she was doing she rushed to the window and frantically waved the lamp up and down. But she knew it was no use. In her haste she had forgotten to arrange a danger signal. She stared out of the window for a few moments then replaced the lamp and sank down on the bed.

* * * * *

One of Thomas's horses snorted, sending a plover screeching away into the darkness. Startled by the sudden noise he looked round to see if the carriage was safe; satisfied, he resumed his vigil, for it was nearly midnight and the signal would come at any moment.

Then he saw it: three flashes of light behind the panes. He picked up his own lamp and swung it to and fro several times. Keeping to the wall he went as far as the yard gate, hoping to meet Elizabeth and help her with her luggage; but beyond that it was dangerous, open ground, so he flattened himself against the trunk of a hawthorn and waited.

Suddenly, to his surprise, he saw another light in Elizabeth's room, only this time it was flickering up and down like a firefly. Puzzled, he stepped away from the shelter of the hawthorn to have a better view, but shrank back again when he heard the sound of barking dogs. Then men came running from all directions, armed with staves and lanterns. He heard a voice he recognised as Mark Edwards's.

"He's out here somewhere. Get him but don't mark him. I want him for myself."

Panic-stricken he retreated along the wall, but three snarling dogs came bounding along the path towards him, pulling a man by a leash. There was a triumphant whoop.

"Here he is, Mark, I've got him."

Thomas backed against the wall and the man malevolently allowed the dogs to snap an inch from his legs. Other men came running and soon he was surrounded. Two of the biggest rushed forward and, in spite of his struggles, pinioned his arms behind his back. Mark Edwards thrust his way forward. When he saw Thomas he grinned.

"Now, my lad! This time you're for it good and proper."

He raised a stave and brought it crashing down on Thomas's head.

"How d'you like that? I've been wanting to do that for a long time."

He lifted the stave again but at that moment the circle parted and Isaac Williams strode forward, panting heavily and carrying a lantern. He went up to Thomas, held the lantern aloft and peered into his face.

"So, Thomas Evans! You'd steal my daughter from under my nose, would you? Pity for you I've got a good nose for varmints, ain't it? Well, varmints must be taught a lesson."

He nodded and Edwards brought the stave down again. The blood poured from Thomas's head over his cheek. Roughly Isaac put his hand under Thomas's chin and forced his head back.

"That's only the start, d'you hear? It's nothing to what you'll get if you come near my daughter again. If I catch you once more on my land I'll have you before me for trespass, and you know what that means, don't you? Transportation for life. And if Mark Edwards here should say, as I've no doubt he will if he's a mind to, that he saw you take a rabbit or a grouse, that means the rope—and as a magistrate I'll see that you get it. So have a care, Thomas Evans, before you come here again."

He nodded once more and the two men pinioning Thomas dragged him along the path to the carriage. They lifted him bodily and flung him in head first. Isaac went up to the carriage and peered down at him.

"So remember! Next time it'll be transportation or the rope—and don't forget, there's plenty of timber in that bloody carpenter's shop of yours that'll go up in flames."

He slapped the rump of the nearest horse, which broke immediately into a gallop, dragging its companion along with it. Soon the carriage was careering down the lane, swaying dangerously from side to side. Isaac watched it until it was out of sight, then glared at the men and went stumping back to the house.

CHAPTER 9

Holding a tray with one hand Janet knocked on Elizabeth's door with the other. There was no reply so she turned the heavy key and went in. Elizabeth was lying on the bed, her face deep in a pillow, still wearing the clothes she had worn on the night of the intended elopement. She did not look up so Janet placed the tray on a table and gently touched her shoulder.

"Oh, Duw, Elizabeth, it do grieve me to see you like this. Don't cry no more, merch fach. It don't do any good in the end."

Elizabeth just shook her head so Janet tried again.

"Your father have let me bring you something to eat at last. You must have something to keep up your strength. You'll be ill otherwise. You've been without food for two whole days now."

"I don't want anything."

"But you must eat, Elizabeth. You'll go to skin and bones if you don't. Your father do want you to dress, too. Mr. Kirkhouse will be here within the hour, and you're to be there to see him, I'm told.

"I shan't see him."

"Of course not, cariad, not if you don't want to. But you must eat even if it's only a little bit. I don't want you becoming ill."

Elizabeth raised her head and stared at Janet with tear-stained eyes.

"How did my father know Thomas was coming here?"

"It was that Mark Edwards who told him. He caught Iestyn going off and became suspicious. He made Iestyn give him the letter to see, then told him to deliver it and not say a word. Iestyn was too twp to know what was going on. They were all lying in wait for Thomas when he arrived."

"What did they do to him? Did they hurt him?"

"Yes. I won't forgive your father for allowing that. Mark Edwards hit him on the head with a stick, then they sent him back in the carriage."

Elizabeth started crying again, her shoulders shaking. Not knowing what else to do Janet sat on the side of the bed, smoothing the fair hair.

"Don't cry, merch fach. There'll be retribution for them all one day for being so cruel, mark my words. But I've got to tell you this, Elizabeth: I'm afraid for Thomas Evans now. The men are saying that your father'll have him arrested if he comes here again and will get him transported for life—and Mark Edwards is going around making jokes about catching him poaching. You know what that lot are like between them. Oh, Elizabeth, I don't think you'd better see Thomas again for his own sake. There's no saying what your father'll do if they catch him trying to see you again."

Elizabeth did not reply. Janet looked around despairingly.

"Oh, Elizabeth, please eat something. Look! I've brought you a drop of cawl and there's some bara brith, too. You always liked that, didn't you?"

"I shall run away," said Elizabeth into the pillow. "I'll go away as far as possible and my father will never see me again."

"There, there! We'll see about that when the time comes. You can always count on me. Now then—"

She reached for the tray but before she could touch it the door burst open and Isaac Williams strode in. He glared at Janet.

"Isn't she up yet? I told you to get her ready."

Janet stood up, scowling.

"She's in no fit state to get up, not after I told her what you did to Thomas Evans."

Isaac pointed at the door with a shaking hand.

"Get out. That's none of your business. I'll speak to you later."

Janet stood her ground and jutted out her chin. For a moment Isaac thought she was going to argue but, at last, muttering under her breath, she shuffled from the room. Isaac went up to the bed and looked down at his daughter.

"Get up, Elizabeth. You know Thomas Kirkhouse will be here shortly."

Elizabeth thrust her face deeper in the pillow.

"I shan't see him. You can't make me."

"Oh, can't I? We'll see about that." Isaac drew up a chair and sat down. "Then it's time you and me had a little chat. Now, my girl, listen carefully. I know you think I'm being hard on you making you marry someone you don't like at the moment, but one day you'll bless me for it. I can see further into the future than you can. I'm not having you throw your life away. You'll be happy with Kirkhouse. He'll give you everything you want and one day you'll have regard and affection for him—then you'll see that what I'm doing is for your own good. You'd never have been happy with that carpenter fellow, although you might think so now. He wouldn't be able to provide for you in the way you've been accustomed to—he'd only bring you misery. You don't see it now, I know, but in a few years you'll be glad I'm forcing you. Then you'll know I was right and you were wrong. I'm not the ogre you're trying to make me out to be. Your concern comes first and foremost with me."

Elizabeth clenched her hands so tightly the knuckles went white.

"You hurt him. You beat him with sticks. I'll never forgive you for that."

"Well, now, he had to be taught a lesson, didn't he? He can't be allowed to come sneaking up here at dead of night to try and snatch you away like a common thief. He'll understand the lesson. He won't bother you again, I promise you that."

Suddenly she slewed sideways, facing him, hatred in her eyes.

"You'll never change, will you, father? You think force and brutality can achieve anything. Is there any wonder everybody around here hates you?"

"Hates me?" He looked genuinely shocked. "I'm not hated. Ask my men. They think very highly of me."

"They would!" She almost spat the words. "They're all as bad as you are. Do you think I don't know what the people say about you? They call you a thief and murderer. I remember the wreck of the *Vainqueur*. You got away with that, didn't you? The enquiry found you not guilty, but did you really steal that cargo and kill those sailors? Did you hit them on the head like you hit Thomas Evans?"

He stared at her, taken back by her vehemence.

"What are you talking about, girl? I've never murdered anyone—sailors or anybody else, and I've never hit Thomas Evans."

"Oh, no! You got Mark Edwards to do it for you, didn't you? You've always had men to do your bidding. That's your trouble. I hate you, just as everyone else does."

Isaac's face darkened.

"You've no right to speak to me like that. The court cleared me of everything years ago—of murder, pilfering and everything else. You know that. You've no right to bring up such things now.''

''Oh, haven't I? The wonder to me is that with a reputation like yours any man wants me at all. What would Mr. Kirkhouse say if he knew the regard you're held in around here? Would he want to marry me then? I think I'd better tell him, don't you?''

''You say anything like that to Kirkhouse,'' said Isaac, speaking as though he suddenly had difficulty in breathing, ''and I'll make you regret it for the rest of your life, see if I don't. I tell you this, Elizabeth: you're going to marry him, come what may.''

''And what if I refuse? What will you do then? Shut me up in this room for the rest of my life?''

''If necessary, but I can tell you this: if you don't wed Kirkhouse I'll damn well make sure you won't get that carpenter. I'll go to any lengths to prevent that. I-I'll hound him out of the country if I have to burn down his bloody shop, if necessary. If you're going to regard me as an ogre I might as well act like one. And I won't guarantee that Mark Edwards won't show his spleen, either. He likes Evans as little as I do. You can take your choice, Elizabeth. Either you marry Kirkhouse or something nasty happens to Evans. You won't see him around here much longer, I can tell you. You've got the alternative in your hands. Think well on it.''

He stood up and went to the door, but turned before reaching it.

''I'll expect you down in half an hour. If you're not there I'll come and fetch you myself. And don't forget—it's either Kirkhouse or the end for Thomas Evans. I'll get him sent to a penal settlement in America before the month is out. I give you my word on that—and I ain't never yet broken a promise.''

He gave her a final glare and went out. This time Elizabeth clenched her hands so tightly the nails cut into the flesh, causing blood to trickle down over the pillow. Then she wept without cease until the sound of carriage wheels told her that Kirkhouse had arrived.

CHAPTER 10

Isaac Williams closed the cow-shed door and pointed to the big south field.

"That's all of six acres. It's fallow now but in the autumn I'll be planting turnips."

Kirkhouse nodded his agreement.

"I have read somewhere that Lord Townshend had a great success with them. He was able to feed his cattle all through the winter, I understand, without killing them off. Perhaps you can do the same."

"I hope so—I hope so. I'm always interested in new ideas."

"Then I expect you've heard of a machine invented by a man called Jethro Tull. A seed drill, I believe he calls it. With a field that size it may be of some use to you."

"Perhaps. But machines cost money."

"Yes, of course, that's the trouble. It's the same in mining."

Isaac led the way into the house. In the banqueting hall he poured a glass of Madeira.

"You'll take some wine, of course."

"Thank you."

Isaac poured a liberal second glass for himself.

"Well, as you can see, there's plenty of potential here. Needs a bit of capital, that's all."

"Yes, that's obvious."

"More stone walling, that's what's wanted. It'll stop that sand. Mind you, a bit of sand ain't to be sneezed at. It lightens the loam. But too much has the opposite effect. Well-built walls will see to that."

"Yes, of course. I'll take your word for it. As a mining engineer I don't know much about farming but I can spot good soil when I see it, and your pasture looks pretty good to me. I've no doubt you could improve on the land, given—as you say—a little capital."

"Quite so. It don't need a lot, but I've already spent more than I can afford on seed and prime cattle. As in every business you have to sink money in before you get a return."

"That's true of mining also. Well, as I told you, I'm only too ready to help."

"You're very generous—very generous indeed. Generous to my daughter, too, if I may say so."

Kirkhouse took a sip of wine.

"Oh, well, you know how I feel about Elizabeth, although I find difficulty in expressing myself in that respect. But you'll not mind my saying that I find it impossible to go long without thinking of her—she rarely leaves my thoughts these days. I would go to great lengths to have her as my wife, as you know, and it's a great encouragement to me to know that you approve of my request for her hand."

"Well, I make no bones about it, Thomas. I liked you the moment I set eyes on you, and that don't happen to many, I can tell you. And when I knew you were interested in Elizabeth I said to myself: now that's a fellar I wouldn't mind having as a son-in-law. It had nothing to do with money, mind, or position. I just like you as a man. I've got to tell you one thing, though: Elizabeth's had quite a number of suitors recently. It's turned her head a bit, I think, and the poor girl don't quite know where she is. So you've got to be careful when you speak to her. Treat her with circumspection, as it were."

"Of course. I always do. It doesn't require a great deal of intelligence on my part to realise how sought after Elizabeth is. She's so beautiful and graceful. I've known her for some time, of course, and she's always been quite amicable with me. A trifle high-spirited, perhaps, but that's to be expected in one so young. But I hope, with kindness and perseverance to show my high regard for her, and so to win her hand."

Isaac slapped him on the back.

"And I'll support you in every way. I've lost no chance already to put in a good word for you, I assure you of that."

"Thank you. That is most kind." Kirkhouse deposited the glass on a table, reached into his breast pocket and took out a rolled parchment. "I have, as you know, briefly outlined a proposal for a dowry. I thought it would be wiser to set out such a proposal formally in a legal document. Then you can see—and I hope Elizabeth will also—that I am in earnest in my request. I can provide for her abundantly—indeed, if I may say so, in a way few other men around here could. Perhaps you'd care to peruse it."

Isaac took the document and read it. He nodded several times.

"Yes, I agree. You've been most generous. As you say, few other men could have provided so well for their intended." He handed the parchment back. "I'm quite sure Elizabeth will be greatly impressed by this."

"I hope so. I know, of course, that having you on my side is half the battle. I would, however, esteem it a favour if you would allow me to see Elizabeth privately—say for an hour or so. It would give me time to express my feelings for her and to outline my proposals. I don't expect an immediate answer, of course, but I feel she has a certain amount of regard for me and then perhaps—"

"Yes, yes, of course. I understand how you feel. Elizabeth would be a fool to refuse you, but don't be too disappointed if your approaches don't have an immediate effect. In some ways Elizabeth is like me—very wilful at times; and I'm quite sure that if you persevere she'll accept you."

"I do hope so. Then would it be possible to see her now, do you think?"

Isaac glanced dubiously upwards.

"Well, yes, I don't see why not. I told her you'd be here, so I expect she'll be down in a moment. If not I'll go and fetch her."

"Oh, please don't hurry her. Truth to tell I'm still pondering in my mind what to say to her. Quite peculiar, really. I can brave any drift or mine—have no fear of an over-hang or fall, or even poison gas—and yet the thought of proposing to Elizabeth makes me an abject coward. Sometimes I am completely lost for words in her presence—"

"Well, I can understand that, but now's the time to take your courage in both hands and put your case forcibly. Tell her you'll marry her, come what may, and show her that dowry. That'll make her realise her good fortune. I've got to warn you about one thing, though: Elizabeth ain't been too well recently. Some disorder she picked up in London. It'll pass but don't expect her to be too full of life or effusive. She's a bit pale these days."

"Oh, I am sorry to hear that. Have you called in the apothecary?"

"No need. It's a temporary malady. She's a bit out of sorts, that's all. Nothing a bit of sea air won't put right. She didn't like London, you know. Too dirty and smelly and Elizabeth's very fastidious."

"Well, I can understand that. I don't care much for London either, so at least we have that in common."

"One other thing. When Elizabeth agrees to marry you—as I'm sure she will—when would you like the nuptials to take place?"

"As soon as possible, if Elizabeth approves. My work is arranged so that I shall be taking a vacation in the autumn, starting in September. That would allow quite a lengthy honeymoon."

"Capital. And where would you like the ceremony to take place?"

"Oh, I thought at Maudlam here. It's your family church, isn't it?"

Isaac's eyes flickered. He put an arm around Kirkhouse's shoulder and lowered his voice.

"Well, yes, but if the truth's to be told, Thomas, I ain't too friendly with the vicar at the moment. He's a bit too high church for me and we don't always see eye to eye. Remember, too, I'm a magistrate and there's one or two miscreants round here who've got it in for me. You know—I've had 'em up in court. I don't care a damn for them, but I wouldn't like my daughter's wedding ruined by shouting or disturbances. See what I mean? Is there any other place you can suggest?"

"Well, of course, if you wish. As a matter of fact I know of a delightful old church near my own home. It's in the village of Llangyfelach, a truly rural setting. I'm sure Elizabeth would like to be married there."

"Capital! Then Llangyfelach it is." Isaac took out his watch. "Well, we'll give her another minute or two. If she ain't down by then I'll send Janet to remind her you're here. Now then, I don't suppose by any chance there'd be coal or minerals under Sker land, would there?"

Kirkhouse smiled and shook his head.

"I doubt it. You see, the main underlying strata is composed of—"

He broke off suddenly for the door had opened and Elizabeth came in. Although forewarned by Isaac he was taken aback by her wan and listless appearance. He recovered immediately and held out his hand.

"Good morning, Elizabeth. I am so pleased to see you."

Elizabeth ignored the hand. She stood quite still, staring unseeingly in front of her. Not knowing what to do Kirkhouse glanced at Isaac.

"Good!" said Isaac. "She's here at last. We'll have another drink on it then I'll leave you both in peace."

He went to the sideboard and poured out three fresh glasses. Kirkhouse was so intent on looking at Elizabeth he did not see Isaac rolling his eyes upwards and muttering a silent prayer of thanks.

CHAPTER 11

MARY WILLIAMS gave a final, deft touch to the chrysanthemums on the sideboard then went to the large bay window to look down the drive. Any moment now the carriage would arrive with Elizabeth and Thomas Kirkhouse, returning from their honeymoon to the big new house in Briton Ferry. It was a pity they had not returned for Christmas and strange that Elizabeth, in her letters, had expressly forbidden any seasonal celebration. Mary sat on a Chippendale chair, delivered only that morning from London, glanced around at the equally sumptuous furniture of the drawing room and sighed. She was envious of Elizabeth. Everything fell into her lap without effort. At all the balls and banquets they had attended it was always her sister who had been the centre of attraction, and now she had captured one of the most eligible men in Glamorgan, rich, influential and capable of giving her everything she desired. Mary would willingly have exchanged places with her.

But envy had not ousted love. Ever since her mother's death she had done her best to look after her younger sister, and now she was worried. Returning from London she had found Sker House full of tension, her father frequently foul-tempered and drunk and Elizabeth withdrawn and distant. It had not taken long to find out why, and immediately she had come down heavily on the side of her father, upbraiding Elizabeth for having become involved with a mere carpenter when Thomas Kirkhouse was there for the asking. As a result the sisters had drawn apart, speaking only occasionally to each other, even during the days of preparation before the wedding.

As she sat waiting Mary's mind went back to the wedding day itself. She remembered it with clarity for it had been her own twenty-first birthday as well—the ninth of September, 1766; but there had been little of the festive about it. Dressing Elizabeth had been like putting clothes on a corpse; she had remained rigid and uncooperative throughout, even when the seamstress was putting the finishing touches to the hem of the heavy, white brocaded gown; and during the long drive to Llangyfelach the three women—Mary, Elizabeth and Janet—had hardly exchanged a word. Indeed, Janet had made things worse, sniffling into her handkerchief all the way there, and only Isaac, who had a bottle in each pocket, had been vociferous with enforced good humour. It was more like a wake than a wedding, and the church had been cold and almost deserted as well, with only the Kirkhouse relatives there. During the ceremony Elizabeth had stared in front of her the whole time, her responses to the vicar barely audible; and at one stage, after looking anxiously at the groom, the Reverend Davies had to prompt her. Then, to cap everything there had been an unfortunate incident at the conclusion of the service. Elizabeth and Thomas had emerged from the church to be stopped by a rope held across the porch by local boys exacting the customary toll; but one of the lads had jerked the rope and dislodged Elizabeth's bouquet. It had fallen to the ground and, either by accident or design, Elizabeth had stepped forward and trodden on it. Mary could see the flowers now, late September roses, crushed and scattered, staining the flag stones red. It was not a good omen for a marriage, and it was to be hoped that the honeymoon had been more successful. The only consolation was that Elizabeth was no longer a distraction to suitors seeking her own hand.

Suddenly she heard the sound of horses and looked up to see the carriage turning in at the drive. She jumped up, rushed out to the hall and flung open the door. She waited for Elizabeth to come up the steps then hugged her.

"Oh, Elizabeth! I'm so glad to see you. You're looking better than when you left."

"Am I?" Elizabeth drew away from the embrace and glanced at Kirkhouse, who was directing the off-loading of the luggage. "I feel a little better, thank you, Mary."

Mary took Elizabeth's arm and led her to the drawing room.

"Did it go well? I mean, was it a good honeymoon?"

Elizabeth threw her cloak across a chair.

"I don't know. What is a good honeymoon?"

"Oh, Elizabeth! Don't sound so miserable. You're in your own home now. I've been looking around. It's a lovely house—the best in Briton Ferry. You're very lucky. You'll be happy here once you've settled down."

"Will I?"

"Of course you will. Now look, Elizabeth. Listen to me before Thomas comes in. I know what the trouble is with you but you must think of the future now, not the past. You have a very loving husband. I think you're very fortunate to have him."

"Am I?"

"Yes, you are. I wish you'd realise it before—"

"He gives me every consideration, if that's what you mean, but I'm no nearer liking him now after three months of his company than before. I don't think I ever shall."

Mary prayed mentally for patience.

"Now you're being unfair. The journey's upset you, that's what it is. In a week or two you'll see things in a different light. You must. Thomas dotes on you. It would be unkind not to respond. It's not many wives whose husbands grant them the slightest wish at the lift of a little finger. Forget the past, I say—forget it before you cause real misery. Forget that Thomas Evans. I know he's the cause of you feeling like this."

Elizabeth's eyes lit up at the sound of Thomas's name.

"How is he? Have you had news of him?"

"No, I haven't." Mary was angry now. "And if I had I wouldn't tell you. Anyway, I never get the time to talk to people, so I wouldn't hear anything about him. I've been more concerned about father. He's been very unwell since you went away."

"Has he?" Elizabeth's voice resumed its disinterested tone.

"Yes, indeed. You must come and see him once you've settled in. He wants to see you. He told me so."

"But I don't want to see him. I shall never set foot in Sker House again."

"Oh, nonsense! I know you and father have had differences—and I know how he wanted you to marry against your wishes. But he thought he was doing his best for you and I agree with him. Which would you prefer? This lovely house or living in a hovel with Thomas Evans!"

Elizabeth did not reply so Mary tried a different approach.

"Tell me about your honeymoon. Where did you go altogether?"

"I can't remember. We travelled a great deal."

"Was there any place you preferred? Tell me about it—tell me all."

"It was tolerable."

"And did you—I mean, did he? Oh, Elizabeth! You know what I mean. I'm dying to know."

"If you mean am I going to have a child, I suppose the answer is yes."

"Oh, I'm so glad. That will make all the difference in the world—to you both. Once you've had a child—"

She broke off as Kirkhouse entered the room. He went up to Mary and kissed her but before he could say anything Elizabeth gathered up her cloak.

"I shall go and change. Will you join us for a meal before you go, Mary?"

"Yes, thank you. I have an hour or so before Mark brings the carriage."

Elizabeth swept out without looking at her husband. He stared after her for a moment then sank into a chair, dejection on his face.

"I've made a mistake there, Mary. I should never have married her. You may as well know that now."

"Oh, nonsense." Mary sat down near him. "Give her time. She'll settle down now that she's back in her own home."

"I doubt it. She's so cold with me. I can't get near her. I do everything I can to please her, but it's no use. I've had three most terrible months. Nothing I do or say is ever right, or is received with complete indifference. I'm to blame, I suppose. I forced myself on her. It's too late to realise that now."

"You mustn't reproach yourself, Thomas. Only a fool would fail to see what a fine, generous man you are, and Elizabeth's no fool, believe me. She'll come round in the end and see your true worth, mark my words. It's still a little soon after—after—"

"That affair with Thomas Evans? Oh, yes, Mary, I know all about that. I've heard all the gossip."

"That was only a passing affair. She'll get over it, especially when she realises what a narrow escape she's had from a life of poverty. Elizabeth hasn't known poverty. When she sees how some of your miners live around here she'll change her mind. Anyway, once you've had a child or two—"

Kirkhouse gave a sardonic laugh.

"A child or two! Do you really think children will make any difference? I have my doubts. I'll let you into a secret, Mary, since we're on the subject of children. Elizabeth did allow me to make love to her on one occasion whilst we were away. For the most part she pleaded sickness, saying she was unwell, but one night I insisted. It was like—like holding a lifeless doll in my arms. It was not repugnance exactly—it was sheer indifference, as though my body meant nothing to her. And afterwards, when she fell asleep, I heard her calling out 'Thomas'. She cried out several times—'Thomas, Thomas'. Like a fool I thought she was calling out for me and when I went to comfort her she opened her eyes then shrank from me. 'You're not Thomas,' she cried. 'You're not my Thomas'. Then she wept without cease until morning. I know now which Thomas she was thinking of. It wasn't me. I see no hope, Mary, no hope at all."

Mary leaned forward and touched his arm.

"Don't despair. It will all come right in the end, I assure you."

"I hope so. I sincerely hope so. I do so love her, Mary, and I've always wanted her, from the very first day we met; but if I'd known things would have been like this—"

"She'll forget Thomas Evans, believe me, then you'll live together happily as man and wife should."

"I'd like to believe you. Quarrelling I could understand, or a show of temper, but not this indifference. That hurts me more than anything. It's—it's even affecting my health, I believe, for sometimes I feel quite unwell. However, you've been a great comfort to me, dear sister-in-law. I'll try and remember what you say and have hope for the future. That's all I can do, anyway. Now don't let's dwell too long on sombre matters. Tell me about yourself. Have you been well? I hear that you were much sought after when you were in London and that you are soon to be married yourself."

Mary laughed.

"It's possible, I think. I seemed to get on quite well with certain—gentlemen there. Three of them asked for my hand so now I must choose, I suppose. One of them is even coming to Sker next week—travelling all the way from London to see me. You must meet him, Thomas, and tell me what you think of him."

"I'll do that willingly if you value my judgement so highly. And your father—how is he?"

"Not well. He's lost his appetite and that's unusual for him. Always he's eaten large meals but now he's just pecking at his food. He's been working too hard on the farm, I believe."

"I must visit him shortly. Perhaps I can bring him a remedy for such a complaint. It's a concoction of rosemary and feverfew and appears to be quite efficacious. I've no doubt it will help him. How's that old housekeeper of yours—Janet?"

"Oh, she's the same as ever. Cheeky and bossy and does the work of a hundred people. She's well over seventy now so I suppose one day—"

She broke off as Myfanwy, the maid, came into the room.

"Yes, Myfanwy?" asked Kirkhouse.

"There's a man here to see Miss Williams, sir," said Myfanwy, curtseying. "He says he's from Sker Manor. Mark Edwards is his name."

"Mark Edwards here already!" exclaimed Mary. "I wasn't expecting him for another hour at least."

"He says he's got an urgent message for you, ma'am. One that can't wait so he came early."

"Then you'd better show him in," said Kirkhouse, rising.

Myfanwy went out and returned immediately with Edwards.

"Well, Mark," said Mary. "Why are you here so soon?"

Edwards twisted his cloth cap in his hands.

"It's your father, miss. He was very unwell last night and this morning we think he's had a bit of a stroke. He's paralysed down one side, Janet thinks. You'd better come as soon as you can."

Mary stood up.

"I'll get ready immediately. You brought the carriage, I take it?"

"Yes, miss, and the horses are still pretty fresh."

"Then wait outside and I'll be with you presently."

Edwards remained where he was, coughing discreetly.

"Yes, Mark," said Mary. "What is it now?"

"I think it best if your brought Miss Elizabeth with you. It's difficult to make out what Mr. Williams is saying but we've heard him calling out several times for her. He seemed kind of agitated about that—so I think she ought to come, too."

"I'll fetch her," said Kirkhouse. "You get ready, Mary. The servants will help you pack."

He took Mary's arm and escorted her from the room. Edwards went after them, still twisting his cap, but at the door he paused and looked back. He stared around at the furniture, gave a low whistle then, grinning, went out to wait by the carriage.

CHAPTER 12

THE SISTERS SPOKE little during the journey to Sker, for their father's illness confronted them with problems they had known would arise one day. Mary, already anxious about his health, was wondering what would happen if he died. There was no-one to take over the lease of the estate which would be sold to another tenant—the highest bidder—and already, she knew, possible applicants, having had wind of Isaac's infirmity, were sounding out the agent. When it came to taking possession of land no speed was lost in farming circles, and instant action could be expected after her father's demise. That meant she would have to leave Sker. Elizabeth had no such problem; she had a home and a husband to turn to but she herself had no-one, unless perhaps the London suitor coming to see her made a firm proposal of marriage. The future was therefore uncertain, although no doubt Thomas Kirkhouse would offer her a place at Briton Ferry. But what she wanted was a home of her own; so she would, she decided, use every weapon in her feminine armoury to capture the Londoner, even if it meant going to live in the Midlands, where he had an estate near a small village called Birmingham.

Elizabeth was also thinking about Sker, but from another point of view. She regarded the house now as a hateful, forbidding place, to be visited only out of necessity; and she felt no compassion for her father even if his illness proved fatal. Coming only three months after her marriage it seemed more like a visitation of God than anything else, a punishment for being so cruel to her. But, whatever the reason, she would show no remorse if he died. Of more importance was the question of Janet's future. Perhaps she could persuade the old housekeeper to return with her to Briton Ferry; it would make life easier to bear if she had Janet to comfort her. If anything happened to her father she would ask her.

Then, as they came to the end of Water Street and climbed the hill leading to the moors, excitement began to well up inside her. They were not far from Newton now, so there was a slight chance she might see Thomas Evans. Eagerly she leaned forward, glancing from left to right in quick succession, but they passed only a few farm-hands and itinerants and there was no one even near the usually populated Town Hall. She sat back again as the carriage turned into Sker drive, more dejected than ever; and, to add to her despondency, the house seemed particulary depressing, its shadow black and long on the frozen soil of the yard. Mary, who had guessed the reason for her sister's animation, said nothing. She dismounted first, aided by Edwards; but Elizabeth ignored his proffered hand and followed Mary into the house.

Janet was in the kitchen as usual, pummelling some dough. She wiped her arms in her apron before embracing Elizabeth and both women shed a few tears. Mary, practical as ever, threw off her coat.

"How's father now, Janet?"

"Failing, I think." Janet blew her nose and glanced meaningfully at Elizabeth. "I think you'd both better go up. I don't know how long he's got on this earth."

The sisters went up to Isaac's room to find him propped up by pillows on the large four-poster bed, his normally ruddy complexion pale and bloodless, a white stubble of beard on his chin. His breathing was shallow and laboured and when Mary took his hand he did not move or open his eyes; but eventually he turned his head and saw her. His breathing quickened and he began to mumble in a choking way, saliva dripping over his paralysed lower lip. Mary leaned forward to hear what he was saying, and after a while seemed to understand. She beckoned to Elizabeth.

"Elizabeth! Father wants to speak to you."

But Elizabeth ignored her. She went to the window and stared out across the moor.

"Elizabeth!" repeated Mary sharply. "Father's asking for you. Please come."

Still Elizabeth did not move. Isaac turned his head slowly to follow the direction of Mary's gaze and a spark of recognition came into his eyes. He released his hand from Mary's, held it up towards Elizabeth and tried to speak, but only a moaning gibberish came out. Suddenly there was a loud, wheezing gasp and the hand fell back on the coverlet. Mary stared for a moment at her father's face then burst into tears.

Elizabeth remained by the window, looking at the moor.

* * * * *

A cold east wind blew among the gravestones of Maudlam cemetery, stirring the clothes of the mourners and rattling the branches of the leafless blackberry bushes. The vicar, his nose red and running, fumbled with the prayer book, his chapped, arthritic fingers protruding from woollen mittens. Few people were at the graveside; only Elizabeth, Mary, Janet and Thomas Kirkhouse, with about a dozen of Isaac's farm-hands standing at a respectable distance among the gravestones, stamping their feet surreptitiously to keep warm.

At last the vicar came to the final passage, intoning the words "ashes to ashes, dust to dust". Kirkhouse, Mary and Janet dutifully picked up handfuls of soil and threw them into the grave, but Elizabeth remained motionless. Seeing this Kirkhouse gathered another handful and gave it to her with a reproachful look. Elizabeth took it automatically and threw it on the coffin, where it spattered over the plaque, obliterating Isaac's name and all the lettering except the last two lines:-

Beloved husband of Catherine
Died 29th December 1766

She stepped back a pace and stared at her mother's tombstone, now lying propped at an angle against the mound of freshly-dug earth. On it the sculptured words, although weathered, could still be made out; and the date seemed to leap out at her: 1st October 1753—thirteen years since her death. How, she wondered, would her mother feel now, seeing Isaac again after all this time, knowing how he had behaved on earth? Would she welcome him with loving arms? They had been happy together once, a long time ago, so perhaps a merciful God would allow them to live together again in a union eradicated of earthly weaknesses. All things were possible in heaven the scriptures said, especially for those who repented; but her father had never shown repentance whilst alive so perhaps he had already been cast down on the Day of Judgement. She herself would never forgive him, even on the day she died.

But before she could delve deeper into such thoughts, the vicar came to the benediction and the farm-hands started singing the wake-hymn 'Diniweidrwydd', their voices thin and reedy against the bitter wind. After a brief, respectful pause Kirkhouse went up to the vicar to thank him and the women made their way slowly along the uneven ground between the graves to the footpath.

"You'll come back with us, won't you?" asked Mary anxiously. "There'll be several things to do—legal things, and I can't see to everything on my own."

Elizabeth nodded. She did not want to return to Sker but she could not refuse such a request. Then, as though forced by some inner compulsion, she looked up. In the distance, beyond the perimeter wall of the churchyard, she could see a familiar figure. It was Thomas Evans. He was staring at her with an expression that was both sad and longing. Elizabeth's heart gave a leap and she took a deep breath, trying to overcome the excitement that had seized her. As though from a distance she heard Mary's voice.

"Come, let's walk to the carriage."

She allowed Mary to take her arm and when they reached the lych-gate she looked back, but there was no sign of Thomas now, and she knew from the demeanour of the others that they had not seen him. Kirkhouse joined them, leading his horse. He held open the carriage door. Before mounting the step Elizabeth turned to him.

"I shall have to remain at Sker for several days now. There will be much to do and I must help Mary. I'll let you know once the legal business has been completed."

Kirkhouse held the lively animal away from the carriage.

"Yes, of course. I understand. Don't hurry things. Make sure the lease is transferred correctly. I don't think the new tenant is in any immediate hurry to take over, but if you have any difficulties let me know. I'll send my own lawyer down."

He waited for Janet to climb stiffly aboard then closed the door and mounted his horse. He waved as the carriage moved off but remained in the same place, pondering. Why, he wondered, had Elizabeth suddenly appeared so flushed and excited as she entered the carriage? He could have sworn she was smiling and there had been something indefinable about her expression, almost as though some new inner radiance had taken possession of her: all very strange in a woman who had not even wanted to come to Sker to attend her father's funeral.

Puzzled, he turned the horse's head towards the Pyle road. He had an appointment at Margam with a man who claimed to have discovered coal near the surface, and he was late already. But as he rode down the hill unease mounted steadily in his mind and when he reached the cottages at Newlands he reined the horse to a halt. He felt inside his pocket and took out the small pistol he always carried when travelling alone and checked the priming. Satisfied, he turned the horse round and rode back along the route he had come. He had thought of a good excuse to return to Sker House.

CHAPTER 13

IT TOOK JANET only a few minutes to put away her top coat and bonnet and roll up her sleeves. With a new zest born of the knowledge that soon she would be leaving Sker to live with Elizabeth in Briton Ferry, she surveyed the shelves of the kitchen.

"Them pans haven't been down for years. I'll boil up the water ready and scour them."

"And I'll go upstairs and start looking around," said Mary. "We've got to decide what to keep and what to sell. Is there anything you want for Briton Ferry, Elizabeth?"

Elizabeth thought for a moment.

"I don't think so. The house is full of furniture as it is. Perhaps a few bits of mother's china, but they can wait until later."

"There's the stock, too," said Mary, "and the implements. Has Morgan Howells said anything about what he wants to buy, Mark?"

"Yes, miss," said Edwards, who had just returned from stabling the horses. "He wants most of it, I think. All the cattle and most of the sheep. He mentioned the ploughs, too."

"Then get the books ready," said Mary. "I'll go over them with you later. We've got to make sure we get the right price for everything."

Mark nodded and went over to the dresser. From a drawer he took several tattered books and laid them on the table. Mary went upstairs but Elizabeth remained standing by the hearth, making no attempt to remove her outer clothes. Janet, who was filling the big iron kettle from the pitcher, glanced up at her.

"I ran a warming pan over your bed this morning, Elizabeth, so it'll be quite aired for you. I knew you'd stay."

"Thank you, Janet. I'll come and help you later. I'm just going for a walk down to the beach."

Janet straightened up so quickly she nearly cracked her head on the chain.

"Now! In this weather! But it's so cold outside. I nearly froze in that cemetery and you will, too, if you go out again."

"Oh, I won't be long. I haven't been near the sea since I left here and I'm longing to see it again. There's plenty of time to do the work over the next few days."

She turned and went out before Janet could say anything more. As the door closed behind her Edwards chuckled.

Janet, uneasy thoughts already coursing through her mind, pretended not to notice and went on filling the kettle, but at last curiosity got the better of her. She swung round on the foreman, now seated at the table, the books spread out in front of him.

"Well, what are you sniggering at?"

Edwards leafed through a ledger before replying.

"You know where she's gone, don't you? It's not the sea she's interested in."

"What d'you mean?" snapped Janet, knowing that her own fears had been voiced.

"I saw Thomas Evans at the cemetery."

"Did you now?" Janet swung the kettle chain round so hard a log went flying to the back of the hearth. "And so now your dirty mind's putting two and two together, I suppose."

"I don't need a dirty mind where she's concerned. She's going to see Thomas Evans, I tell you."

Janet put her hands on her hips, striking a pose of anger and contempt to hide her anxiety.

"Nonsense! She wouldn't do a thing like that now she's married. Before, perhaps, but not now. Anyway, you've done enough harm there, Mark Edwards. You mind your own business."

"And you mind yours when you get to Briton Ferry, Janet fach, or you won't last long, I can tell you."

"Diawch!" For once Janet was lost for words. "I'll be glad to see the last of you. It's a wonder to me Morgan Howells is keeping you on here."

Edwards grinned and reached for another book,

"Well, he is, and if you ask me it's a good gaffer he's getting."

Janet shook her head helplessly and went to the window. But all she could see from there was the corner of the cowshed and part of the brown earth of the south field.

* * * * *

Elizabeth walked along the path to Pwll Dafan, sedately at first in case anyone was watching, then more quickly when she thought she was out of sight of the house; and when she came to the final rise she broke into a run. She knew without doubt that Thomas would be at the cove; it was as though their minds had communed in that one quick instant at the cemetery. He would be there without fail. Breathless, she reached the top of the promontory and stared around, trying to catch a glimpse of him through her wind-blown hair, remembering too late that she had forgotten her bonnet.

Then she saw him, as she knew she would, standing by the entrance to the cove. She ran to him and flung herself into his arms; and they clung together, kissing hard and fiercely, oblivious of the wind cutting into their faces. Then, as breathless as she, Thomas drew her into the shelter of the cove; and, without speaking, they lay down on the sand. He kissed her again and without hesitation searched with one hand among her voluminous underclothes, trying to find her body, anxious for them to be joined together. As eager as he, and knowing how little time they had, she helped him as best she could; and so intent were they on reaching the culmination of their love they failed to hear the sound of a horse galloping furiously along the drive to Sker House.

* * * * *

Thomas Kirkhouse re-passed Maudlam church at a canter, noticing that the cemetery was now deserted save for two grave-diggers busy at their task of re-filling the grave. Ever since leaving there a short while ago he had visualised Elizabeth's face as she entered the carriage, remembering in every detail her strange, unusual expression. It was wrong for a husband to think evil of his wife, but he could not help himself, and he had already heard too many rumours for comfort. Hating himself for what he was doing he waited for the horse to reach flat land then kicked it into a gallop, tearing down the road at break-neck speed, not even slacking pace as he turned into the rut-infested track of Sker House.

Reaching the yard he pulled up in a violent, slithering halt, flung the reins over a post and pushed open the kitchen door. A startled Janet confronted him, her hands in a large iron pot; but Mark Edwards, sitting at the table, seemed less surprised by his sudden entry. Kirkhouse slapped a boot with his crop.

"Where's Mrs. Kirkhouse?"

Janet's hands flew to her breast.

"Oh, Duw! I don't know. Around here somewhere, I suppose. We didn't think we'd see you for another few days, Mr. Kirkhouse."

"I dare say," said Kirkhouse drily. "I've brought some papers Mr. Williams gave me some time ago. They'll be needed for the settling up. I meant to give them to Mrs. Kirkhouse at the funeral but I forgot. Is she upstairs?"

Janet became even more flustered.

"I don't know. I don't think so. I'll go and look, shall I?"

"No, don't bother." Kirkhouse strode towards the inner door. "I'll go myself. She can't be far. You've not been long in, have you?"

"No, not long," said Janet weakly.

Kirkhouse reached the door and was about to open it when Edwards stood up and gave a cough.

"I know where Mrs. Kirkhouse is, sir."

"Do you? Well! Where?"

"She's down at the beach," said Edwards. "She's gone to a cove near an inlet called Pwll Dafan."

Kirkhouse stared unbelievingly at him.

"Now? On a day like this? Why should she want to go there, for heaven's sake?"

Edwards coughed again.

"It's one of her favourite places, I think."

"How do I get to this—this cove?"

"You take the path past the stable and go towards the sea. It leads right there. You can't miss it. It's only about three hundred paces."

Kirkhouse glanced suspiciously at him, murmured a "Thank you" and went out. Janet looked venomously at Edwards.

"You devil, you! If you thought Thomas Evans was down there why did you send him? Do you know what you're doing?" Her voice became shrill.

Edwards resumed his seat and opened another book.

"Telling the truth, that's all. That's where he'll find her, and the best of luck to all of them."

He laughed and went on reading, but Janet ran again to the window, twisting her hands together in anguish. Then, feeling faint, she sat down on the rocker and rocked furiously, her lips moving silently in prayer.

CHAPTER 14

JANET HAD JUST summoned enough courage and energy to start on another pot when the door flew open and Elizabeth was almost flung into the room. After her came Thomas Kirkhouse, scowling, his face the colour of parchment. Elizabeth, in tears, looked appealingly at Janet and moved towards her, but Kirdhouse seized her roughly by the wrist and pulled her towards the inner door. As it closed behind them Edwards leaned back in his chair and laughed raucously; but Janet, still holding her breast, went to the door to listen. She heard Elizabeth being dragged along the hall and a moment later the door of the banqueting room slammed shut. Knowing that further work was impossible she retreated once more to the rocker.

In the banqueting room Kirkhouse pointed to a chair.

"Sit down, Elizabeth. I must talk with you."

She replied by turning her back on him. Breathing heavily from exertion and shock at what he had just witnessed, Kirkhouse fought to retain a semblance of calm.

"I know you've never loved me, Elizabeth—I've known that from the very beginning—and I know about your affair with that—that man; but I never thought you'd stoop to this. Not now! Not after your marriage vows. Don't they mean anything to you—anything at all?"

For a moment Elizabeth did not move, then she swung round viciously on him.

"Marriage vows! What marriage vows? Forced vows, you mean. I never wanted to marry you in the first place, and you know it, so don't talk to me about vows."

Kirkhouse's resolve to be firm wilted suddenly under her vehemence. He began to stutter.

"B—but I thought by now, surely—"

"You thought what? That you'd spy on me? That's what you were doing, wasn't it? Coming down here after saying you were going to Margam—with the pretext of a few papers—and then threatening Thomas Evans with a pistol! Why, he's worth a hundred of you. I'd go to him now if I could."

She turned her back on him again, making him feel helpless.

"I never had any intention of shooting him," he said lamely. "I just wanted to frighten him, that's all. Indeed, I find it difficult to blame him. Loving you as much as I do I can understand how he feels—he wants you as much as I do. But I do blame you, Elizabeth. You're married to me now and—"

"Yes." The word came in a hiss. "I'm married to you, and how I rue the day I was."

"I also. But surely—to meet that man now—on the very day your father is buried! I just can't understand it! Why, only an hour ago you saw his coffin being lowered into the ground—"

"And was I glad to see it go! I hated him as much as I do you. You were in league together."

He shook his head desperately.

"You shouldn't speak of the dead like that, especially your own father. Surely now that death has interceded—"

Once more she rounded on him.

"Didn't it strike you as strange that so few people were at the funeral? If my father had been respected the church would have been full to overflowing. Everybody around here hated him as much as I did. And has it never entered your head that's why we were never married at Maudlam? Oh, no, it didn't! It was only you who didn't appear to know that—or if you did you chose to ignore it."

"I didn't hate your father," he said almost in a whisper. "It's true we were in league over my wanting to marry you—I admit it. I let my love for you blind me, like the fool I was. I blame myself now, not your father—or even Thomas Evans. But it grieves me to know that you feel like this about me. I've never done anything to deserve such vituperation."

She laughed mirthlessly.

"It's good of you not to blame Thomas Evans, anyway."

He sat down as though his legs had suddenly become weak, and held his temples with trembling hands.

"I don't know what to do now, that's the trouble. Soon this place will be taken over by a new tenant. Mary will be married and go away to live. You have no other home but Briton Ferry. And yet we cannot live together. It's impossible to go on like this. I've never known such unhappiness."

"You brought it on yourself—and on me, too."

"I see that now. But it doesn't solve the problem of what we must do."

"What is there to do? I'm married to you, as you so constantly remind me, so we must live together in misery for the rest of our lives."

"Oh, dear God, no!" He transferred his hands to his eyes, covering them. "Surely not. Surely you could try and have a little regard for me, Elizabeth. Couldn't you forgive me for—for having forced myself on you? It wouldn't be easy, I know, but if only you tried. I would do all in my power to please you, I assure you of that. Then, perhaps, we could have some normalcy of existence. As it is we cannot go on as we are, that's for certain."

"No, we cannot go on as we are."

"But whatever the outcome I must ask you not to see Thomas Evans again. You must promise me that. I will not allow you to."

"And what will you do if I refuse? Lock me in my room as my father did?"

He stared blankly at her.

"No. I'm sorry to hear that. I didn't know he'd done such a thing. If I had known I—I'd have prevented him somehow. I merely ask you, on your word of honour, not to see Thomas Evans again."

She stood over him, looking scornfully down on the bowed head.

"And that I cannot and will not promise. However, if it's any consolation to you I'll tell you this: I will not consciously seek Thomas out, for I am married to you, as you say, and the bible forbids it. But if ever I meet him by chance I cannot guarantee what will happen, for you will never quench the love I have for him. That's the most I will promise."

"Then that's some consolation, at least," he said dully. "I pray you will not meet him too often."

"Very well. And in return I ask you for a promise also—that you will not spy on me again. I will not stand for spying—by you or anybody else. Is that understood? Well, will you promise?"

He nodded, all courage gone.

"Yes, I promise. I'm sorry. My feelings ran away with me today. I admit I came here to search for you. I was consumed by jealousy and I couldn't stop myself. I won't do it again."

"Then let us have an understanding," she drove home. "As far as the outside world is concerned we shall appear to live together amicably, but in actual fact we will go our separate ways. I've said that I'll not meet Thomas Evans again of my own volition, but neither will you be suspicious of me or spy on me. I want complete freedom to go where I will and do as I wish. Those are my conditions. Is it agreed?"

"Yes," he said miserably. "I agree. I have no alternative, have I? But I must ask you one thing, Elizabeth, and I want to know the answer now. Are we to have children? You know I would dearly like a son and heir, and if we do then, perhaps—"

"Why do you ask that now?" she said sharply. "You know very well that in all probability I am already with child—your child."

"Then I thank God for it. Perhaps if we could have a son—or even a daughter—the future would be easier to bear. Perhaps it will be some form of bond between us. I can only hope so."

She sat down at last, heavily.

"A very loose bond, I assure you. However, never fear—I shall be a good mother to your child, rest assured on that score. Then it is arranged. We go our separate ways and you will not keep watch on me, even for one instant."

"Yes, it's arranged."

There was silence for a moment as Kirkhouse tried to fight back his tears. Then, suddenly and impetuously, he went towards her and knelt down in front of her. He placed his head on her lap and pressed his hands into her thighs, running them up and down the smooth, firm contours.

"Oh, Elizabeth. Can't I make you understand how much I love you? You'll never be able to stop me doing that. You mean everything in the world to me. I love your hair, your eyes—your body. I would do anything in the world to make you love me in return; and perhaps, God willing, one day you will. Please say there's a chance that at least you'll try. Please, Elizabeth, please say that."

She looked down at him, unmoved.

"You would be foolish to have such thoughts. Let us be content with our promises to each other."

Kirkhouse nodded but kept his head in her lap, afraid to let her see his tears, but glad also that he was allowed to remain there, if only for a moment. Elizabeth stared in front of her, trembling herself now. She had won a victory but at great cost. Never again, she knew, would either of them find happiness.

FINALE

CHAPTER 1

ELIZABETH SAT IN the drawing room of the Briton Ferry house reading to her eldest son, George Bedlington, aged nine. The story was about a fox and George, although he had heard it a dozen times before, was still enthralled. He sighed when Elizabeth came to the end and closed the book.

"He was a naughty animal, wasn't he, Mama?

"Indeed he was, Georgie. A sly, crafty old animal if there ever was one."

"Will you read me some more?"

"Not now. It's time for bed. Your little brothers must be fast asleep by now. I've let you stay up only because it's Christmas and you're older than they are—and because you're coming shopping with me to Swansea market tomorrow."

"Can I help to choose the presents?"

"Of course. We'll choose them together."

"What will Papa be having?"

"Oh, I think he'd like a pair of slippers. Come along then. Off with you."

George pulled a face.

"Can I warm myself by the fire first? The bedroom is so cold."

"Five minutes, then. That's all."

George clambered off the settee and stood by the fire, looking up at the garlands of holly, mistletoe and ivy on the mantelpiece. He seemed very small by the tall hearth, hardly bigger than he had been a year ago, and Elizabeth's mind went back to the day he was born. He had always been a frail child, and the delivery had been difficult, an ordeal repeated a year later when a second son had died in infancy. Afterwards the births of Thomas and William had been easier, but she had resolved to have no more children, which was a good excuse not to have Thomas Kirkhouse share her bed. He still came to her occasionally to allay gossip among the servants, but his visits had become less frequent over the years, a fact that pleased her, for she still felt repugnance at his touch. Ruefully she thought of the last nine years and of their promises to each other.

She had broken her word only twice when, hearing that Thomas Evans was giving recitals at the Town Halls of Aberafon and Neath, she could not resist the temptation of going to hear him; but each time the venues had been crowded, with little chance of meeting him, so in a way she had kept her part of the bargain, although not a day went by without her thinking of him and remembering their last few moments together. Even the birth of her children had not prevented that; indeed they only served to remind her of what might have been. Her husband had kept his word, too, never once questioning her whereabouts and concealing any suspicion he may have entertained. In that respect his place had been taken by his parents who, sensing her aloofness towards their son, had become resentful of her treatment of him. Indeed, there were times when their dislike bordered on hostility, and she had come to dread their visits to the house, now also mercifully less frequent. Looking back, the nine years had been more than wasted: they were an aeon of time without happiness or hope, with nothing to look forward to but the bitterness and recriminations of old age.

Still deep in thought she reached for the bell-cord, intending to end George's period of grace, but as she was about to pull the thong she heard the sound of carriage wheels on the drive, and a few moments later the door burst open to reveal the flushed, excited face of her sister.

"Surprise, surprise," shouted Mary. "You didn't expect to see me in Briton Ferry, did you?"

Elizabeth jumped to her feet in time to meet Mary's embrace.

"Mary! What on earth are you doing here? I thought you were in Birmingham."

"We were," Mary laughed, "but Andrew had some business in Aberafon, so we came down here. I rushed on post-haste to ask you if we could stay with you over Christmas."

"Of course you can. You're very welcome, as you always are. I'll call Janet and get the bed aired for you."

"Oh, there's no hurry." Mary loosened her coat. "We shall be staying the night at Aberafon, and I must return there immediately or Andrew will be angry. But we'll be here tomorrow. And how is Master George Bedlington? Dear me! It must be at least a year since I saw him last. Are you quite well, Georgie?"

"Quite well, thank you, Aunt Mary," said George, kissing her.

"And how are the other children, Elizabeth?"

"Fairly well. Thomas had the croup last month and William has been down with chicken pox. But they're both fully recovered, I'm glad to say."

Mary rubbed her muff in George's cheek.

"How time flies! It seems only a short time ago that George was hardly able to crawl, and now he's a real little gentleman."

"Gentleman enough to go to bed," said Elizabeth. "He was on the point of going when you came. Georgie, go down to the kitchen and tell Janet your Aunt Mary is here, but don't come back until she's dressed you for bed."

"Can't I stay up a little longer now that Aunt Mary's here," said George, pouting.

"No," said Elizabeth firmly. "Aunt Mary and I have lots to talk about before she returns to Aberafon. She only has a few minutes. Off you go."

George reluctantly kissed his mother and aunt and set off for the kitchen. The sisters sat down on the settee.

"I really mustn't stay long," said Mary. "I promised Andrew I'd be back within the hour. So Janet's still alive, then."

"Very much so, although she's over eighty now—eighty-five, I think. She's not sure herself."

"And does she still like it here with you?"

"I believe so. She's still as abrupt as ever, though. Janet will never change."

Mary looked her sister up and down.

"You're a little thinner than when I saw you last. Haven't you been well?"

"Well enough, I suppose. I've been troubled with a cough recently—it seems to persist in the cold weather. I expect it will go when the spring comes."

"Look after yourself now, for the sake of the children. Oh, how I envy you those three. They're the loveliest children I've ever seen and we haven't one. It distresses me a great deal."

"Don't worry about it." Elizabeth tried to put conviction into her voice. "There's plenty of time. You'll have children one day, I'm sure."

"I do hope so. It isn't for the want of trying, I assure you. Andrew's quite insatiable. He's like a bull sometimes, especially after he's had too much to drink. But so far, nothing's happened. He's beginning to blame me, I think."

"Well, I'm sure you'll be lucky one day."

Mary gave her sister a quick, penetrating glance.

"Mind you, I'm like you in some ways. I can get anything out of him. He makes money hand over fist with various stocks and shares. I think he wants to talk to Thomas about that—he's thinking of putting some money into coal mines, so they'll be discussing business all over Christmas, I expect. How is Thomas, by the way?"

"Quite well. I don't see much of him. He's away most of the time—sinking some new shaft or other."

"Are you happy now? Happier than you were, I mean?"

"Tolerably so, I suppose. We don't quarrel, if that's what you mean."

"I don't mean that. I mean—well, you must live happily to a certain extent. You've got three children to prove it."

Elizabeth looked down at her hands, lightly clasped in her lap.

"We share the same bed occasionally and pretend to act normally, and I don't resist when he wishes to make love to me. But I still don't love him."

"Well, you never did, did you? You've always been honest about that. Do you still hanker after that—that Thomas Evans?"

Elizabeth turned her head away.

"I'd rather not discuss Thomas Evans."

"Oh, Elizabeth. Surely after all this time you must realise that he'd have been no good for you. He was a nice enough man, I suppose, but he was just a harpist—a sort of wandering minstrel, wasn't he? You'd never have been able to live the sort of life he'd have led you."

"I never had the chance to try, did I?"

"Oh, Elizabeth! I thought you'd have been wiser by now."

Elizabeth did not reply so Mary changed her tactics.

"Mind you, I hear he's making quite a name for himself. He plays at the best balls and banquets, I'm told, and he's a regular visitor to Nottage Court. The Blundells are his patrons, I believe."

"Thomas is no ordinary musician," said Elizabeth dully. "He's very talented. One day the world will know that."

"Oh, I've no doubt, if you say so. Have you seen him recently?"

"No."

"A good thing, too. I heard you went to hear him at Neath a year or two back. I hope you've stopped doing silly things like that now."

Again Elizabeth did not reply.

"Well, as long as you have," Mary went on briskly. "I thought once he'd have ruined your marriage before it even started. There was that awful affair down at Sker, wasn't there, just after—"

"Mary! Please! I'd rather not discuss it."

"Very well, I'll say no more. Have you tended father's grave recently?"

"No."

"Then I'll go myself. Probably on Boxing Day. Will you come with me?"

"No."

"Oh, Elizabeth! You are hard. Don't you ever think of the happy times we had at Sker?"

"I remember the happy times very well. I prefer to forget the unhappy ones."

"Well, we'll have a long talk about the good times over Christmas. Which bedroom are we having? The front one?"

"Yes. The same as last time."

"Good. I like the bed in that room. Andrew does, too. Perhaps we'll conceive there this time. You never know."

In spite of herself Elizabeth laughed.

"Indeed, I hope you will."

Mary stood and buttoned her coat.

"Well, I must go. We'll be here just before dinner tomorrow night. You've enough food, I suppose, for Andrew. He eats like an ox, as you know."

"Oh, yes. There's plenty. The larders are groaning with stuff. What would Andrew like for Christmas, do you think? I'll get him something in Swansea tomorrow."

"Oh, don't bother. He's got just about everything he wants. I can't think what to get him myself. Probably a cravat. I give him one every year. If you could get him some walnuts, perhaps, he'd be delighted. He's very partial to those."

"Then I'll try and get walnuts."

They went to the door and there met Janet and George, now wearing his night-shirt. Smiling up at them, his fair hair freshly brushed, he looked very like Elizabeth. Mary picked him up and hugged him.

CHAPTER 2

George kept a tight hold on his mother's skirt as they made their way through the crowds at Swansea market. Elizabeth's bag was full of chestnuts and small presents for the servants; and a quick consultation with her list told her that she had purchased everything except laver-bread. This she was determined to get, for it was a delicacy she and Mary had enjoyed since their days at Sker when they collected seaweed from the rocks. Living far inland now her sister would enjoy it as a special treat, fried with thick slices of bacon on Christmas morning. She pushed her way through to the front of a cockle and laver-bread stall and began examining the tubs to ensure that the black, shiny fronds were free of sand and properly cooked.

But as she was opening her purse and about to select a coin she heard a sound that made her forget the purchase. Above the shouts and hubbub of the market place the faint, tremulous notes of a harp came to her. Ignoring the enquiring glances of the cockle-woman she turned to listen, then heard a man's tenor voice as well, singing an air she had never heard before. Suddenly she felt a clenching in her stomach. There was only one voice like that in the world. She dropped the coin back in the purse, took George's hand and drew him away from the stall.

For a few moments she stood in the narrow passageway, buffeted by the hurrying shoppers, trying to make out the source of the sound. It seemed to come from somewhere near the market entrance so, pulling George, she half ran, half walked to the end of the stalls, then along an alley leading to the street. There she was slowed by supplicating beggars and pedlars, but she fought her way onwards, the music becoming louder with every step.

Then she could go no further. A crowd of people blocked the end of the alley. Sitting or standing on the steps that led down to the street they were listening intently. She stood on tip-toe, craning for a view, but could see nothing, but she could hear Thomas's voice clearly now, singing an air so beautiful and plaintive she was suddenly filled with a strange and ineffable sadness. He was singing in Welsh and the words, although she could not understand every one, made her catch her breath.

Mab wyf fi sy'n byw dan benyd,
Am f'anwylyd fawr ei bri,
Gwaith ei charu fwy na digon
Curio wnaeth fy nghalon i.
Gwell yw dangos beth yw'r achos
Nag ymaros dan fy nghur,
Dere'r seren—

He broke off suddenly, as though overcome by the poignancy of his own music, and there was a sympathetic murmuring from the onlookers. Frantic to see him Elizabeth noticed a small gap between the nearest people and the wall, so she pushed herself forward, dragging George with her. By leaning sideways she could just see Thomas's head and shoulders, and with a shock she realised that he had aged and that his eyes were full of tears. She shrank back against the wall, trembling, a dull ache mounting steadily in her breast. Then, just as faintness was about to overcome her, he began again in English.

Slight me not, my only treasure,
Trust me, maid I fondly love;
View each rural spot with pleasure,
Where my charmer designs to rove,
Fears all hushing,
Sweetly blushing,
Come thou fairest theme of song;
Love assists me,
Nought resists me,
Bars and bolts can't hold thee long.

She knew now without doubt. The song was for her, and the bitter irony of the words, accentuated by every plaintive, haunting note, stabbed into her like a knife. She could contain her grief no longer. Clinging to George for support she wept uncontrollably; and George, certain now that some dreadful calamity had befallen them, started crying, too. A few people turned to stare and one, an old woman balancing a basket of fish on her head, put an arm on her shoulder.

"Beth sy'n bod gyda ch'i, merch?"

But Elizabeth ignored her. She picked up George and ran blindly out of the market place, and did not stop until she reached the waiting carriage.

* * * * *

Watched by Myfanwy, Janet vigorously stirred a saucepan of broth. When it was at the desired consistency she ladled some of it into a soup dish and cut a piece of bara gwenith. Myfanwy could hide her curiosity no longer.

"What's the matter with Mrs. Kirkhouse, Janet? She looked like a ghost when she came back from Swansea just now and she rushed straight up to her bedroom without even taking her cloak off."

Janet did not answer. Instead she placed a cover over the dish and set out some Welsh cakes on a plate.

"Poor little Georgie was crying, too," Myfanwy persisted. "He looked as pale as a sheet and Mr. Kirkhouse had to take him into the drawing room and let him take his play-box out to console him. Has something dreadful happened?"

Janet still ignored her. She placed the soup dish and plate on a tray and covered both with a napkin.

"Open the door, Myfanwy, and don't talk so much."

Myfanwy opened the door.

"I don't think she'll touch any of that. When I was up there just now she was still fast asleep—or she seemed to be, anyway."

"Taw sôn, girl. Just hold the door open."

Janet brushed past her into the hall and there met Thomas Kirkhouse coming down the stairs. He glanced dubiously at the tray.

"I'm going to send for McTavish. He's a better physician than that bumbling old Evans. All he can say is that he thinks it's some kind of shock or swoon, but I've never known a swoon last as long as this."

"I'll try her with some food," said Janet. "If I can get her to eat she'll feel better."

"Well try, by all means, but she's still in a sort of coma. I can't get her to say anything, even to me. I can't understand it. I've questioned the groom. They had no accident coming back from Swansea, so there was nothing to upset her that I know of. George said that she started crying in the market, but he doesn't know why. It's a mystery to me why this should have come on so suddenly."

"Then you fetch the other doctor and perhaps we'll have some sense around here. I'll go and stay with her.

Kirkhouse nodded and Janet hobbled up the stairs. Elizabeth was lying as she had left her, her face framed by her fair hair and the pillow. Her eyes were closed and her cheeks still stained from weeping. Janet placed the tray on a table and bent over her.

"I've brought you some cawl, cariad," she whispered. "If you wake up and eat some it will do you good."

For a long while there was no response, but at last Elizabeth opened her eyes. They rested on Janet but she said nothing.

"Oh, Duw, cariad!" cried Janet. "There's glad I am you've woken up at last. Are you feeling better now? You've given us all a fright around here. I've never seen you like this before. Do you feel ill in yourself? Look—I've brought some cawl for you. I've been keeping it warm ever since you got back from Swansea. If only you took it, it would build you up."

Elizabeth did not reply immediately. When at last she spoke her voice was low, almost inaudible.

"Soon the snow will come, Janet. I don't want to see the snow."

Janet did not hear properly. She stooped lower.

"What did you say, merch fach? I didn't catch what you said."

"Soon the snow will come. I don't want to see it again. I shall die before it comes."

Janet straightened up, aghast.

"Oh, Duw! What are you talking about, girl? You're not going to die. Nobody around here's going to die. Don't talk such nonsense."

Elizabeth just shook her head.

"Now don't say things like that," scolded Janet. "What have caused you to feel like this? You were all right this morning. What have happened since then? You can tell old Janet."

"I just want to die, Janet. I don't want to live any more."

Janet became angry, but only because of fright.

"For shame on you saying things like that. What would the children think if they heard you? Do you want to upset them?"

"Forgive me, Janet. Look after them for me, will you, as long as you can. Tell them I loved them."

"Oh, Elizabeth! What nonsense are you talking about? Mr. Kirkhouse have sent for a new doctor. You'll feel better when he comes. Just wait till then."

"I don't want a doctor. I shan't see him."

Elizabeth sighed and closed her eyes. Thoroughly alarmed now, Janet looked around in desperation. She ran towards the door and as she reached it Kirkhouse came in.

"I've sent for McTavish," he began, then caught sight of Janet's expression. "What's the matter?"

"Oh, Mr. Kirkhouse!" cried Janet. "There's glad I am you've come. She's been talking about dying. She don't want to live, she says, and won't see the doctor. I was coming to tell you."

Kirkhouse looked past her at Elizabeth, then went up to the bed and sat down on a chair. He took one of Elizabeth's hands in his.

"Elizabeth! What's the matter? What's happened to make you feel like this? George has been asking about you. He wants to see you. He's been worried about you."

There was no response. Kirkhouse glanced at Janet and shook his head.

"This is beyond me. She appeared quite well this morning. She went to Swansea in a fairly happy mood, I thought. She ate a normal breakfast and she was looking forward to her sister staying here. She's had a bit of a cough recently, I know, but it's beyond my comprehension why this should have come on so suddenly."

He went on holding Elizabeth's hand but, although he was worried, he showed no sign of great distress. Nine years of indifferent marriage had taken their toll on him. But he still loved his wife and so he bowed his head in prayer, and beside him Janet's lips moved, too. Then, faintly, they heard Elizabeth's voice and both bent forward to hear what she was saying.

"Sing it for me, my dearest. Sing it always for me."

"What did she say?" asked Janet. "I couldn't hear what she said."

"I'm not sure," said Kirkhouse uneasily. "Something about singing, I think."

Then, as they watched, two large tears welled out from under Elizabeth's eyelids and coursed down her cheeks. They heard her again.

"Oh, Thomas, stay with me a little longer, my darling. Stay with me until the snow comes."

Kirkhouse glanced at Janet and stood up. His expression had hardened.

"I'll get McTavish. There's nothing I can do for the moment."

Janet nodded and sat in the vacated chair. Now Elizabeth was weeping continuously and silently, the tears trickling down even as far as the pillow. Janet took out a handkerchief and wiped them away, then smoothed back the long, fair hair with gentle, sweeping strokes, just as she had done when Elizabeth was a child. Slowly, inexorably, a dark, abysmal fear grew within her and she began to shiver. Long acquainted with death in all its forms she could detect its stifling presence in the room.

CHAPTER 3

THE SNOW WAS falling steadily as Janet's carriage went at a brisk pace along Moor Lane towards Newton. To her right she could see the outlines of Nottage, the buildings black against the white world that seemed to engulf everything, and she was glad that her journey was nearly over. With luck she would be able to return to Briton Ferry before the roads became impassable.

Soon the carriage was swaying between stone-built cottages and she saw the sombre outline of Newton church. They came to a halt outside a barn-like structure, where the driver dismounted and lowered the steps for her. Stiffly she climbed down, saw a split-level door, knocked and walked in. Thomas Evans was desultorily planing a piece of wood. He looked up as she entered, his face heavy with grief. He lowered the plane on a work-bench.

"I know why you've come, Janet. I've been waiting for you. Elizabeth's dead, isn't she?"

Janet sat down heavily on a trestle.

"Yes, but how did you know? She died just after midnight."

"I was with her when she died. She came to me in my dreams."

Janet nodded slowly several times.

"She went peaceful in the end. She said she'd go when the snow came and it started before midnight. Less than a fortnight she's been ill altogether."

"I pray to God that I'll die soon so that I can be with her."

"No!" The word exploded like a pistol shot. "You mustn't speak like that. That's what I've come to tell you. She knew you'd say that but she said you must go on living—to forget her now and forgive her for the misery she's caused you—that you mustn't grieve for her any more."

"She caused me no misery, Janet. The only misery I had was because I couldn't possess her. Every moment I spent with her—few though they were—were nothing but happiness. I shall always grieve for her."

Janet reached for a handkerchief and blew her nose noisily.

"It do do me good to hear you speak like that, but she was adamant about me telling you. Forget her now, she said, and find a good woman who'll be kind to you and marry her. Make him marry, Janet, she said, and see that he settles down with somebody who'll love him and comfort him. That was her express wish."

Thomas drew up a stool and sat down beside her.

"I'll not marry, Janet. Elizabeth's memory is all I want now until my own time comes."

"Well, that's what she told me to tell you, and so now I have. And she had another wish, too—a very special one. She mentioned it several times before she died. She wants you to go on singing that song you composed for her—the one you sang in Swansea market."

He stared at her.

"She heard me in Swansea market! When?"

"Just before Christmas. She saw you there singing to some people. It was just after coming back from there that she took to her bed."

"Oh, God! Why didn't she speak to me?"

"I don't know. She was with her son, so perhaps she didn't want him to know about you."

"But if only she'd spoken to me, Janet. Perhaps then she wouldn't have died."

"Perhaps. I don't know. All I do know is that she pined away after coming back from there and hearing you sing that song. She didn't want to live after that, even for the children. There was nothing else wrong with her as far as I could make out, except a bit of a cough. She always pined for you, mind—I know that—but it was the song that finished her, I think—she kept on talking about it and crying because she couldn't be with you. But don't reproach yourself, Thomas. You weren't to know that, and I know how much she loved you. I don't approve of what went on between you, mind—not after she married, that is—but I'm not blaming you. Anyway, I've told you all she asked me to, and I've done my duty. The funeral will be at Llansamlet on Monday. Will you be there?"

"No, Janet. I'll go later when there are no people about. I want to be alone with her."

Janet struggled painfully to her feet.

"I thought you'd say that and it's for the best. Well, I shan't be long for this world myself. I shan't be sorry to leave it, especially now that Elizabeth's gone. I've seen much happiness but a lot of misery, too—and I don't want no more misery. I've had enough of it."

She turned to go, then paused.

"Remember about that song, Thomas. Elizabeth was adamant about it. Sing it, she said, as often as you can and wherever you can—at all the mabsantau you go to, if possible—and then she'll be happy wherever she is. You must do that in memory of her. It was her very last wish before she died. She said that one day even her grave will disappear, and people will walk over where she's buried without remembering her—but your song will go on forever—and that's how she wants to be remembered. Those were her very last words, so see that you obey them. If you don't everything between you will have been in vain, won't it?"

She shuffled out, leaving Thomas staring at the floor. After a while he lifted his head and looked around for his harp, now lying discarded in a corner among the shavings. Then he turned to the work-bench in front of him. On it, now finished and polished, was the love spoon he had once made for Elizabeth.

CHAPTER 4

Except for an area around Elizabeth's grave where the mourners' feet had churned an ugly, brown slush, the cemetery of Llansamlet parish church lay under six inches of snow. The grave itself, its pristine whiteness contrasting sharply with the defiled earth around it, seemed to emphasise the solitude of the burial ground, empty now save for one person. Thomas Evans, his dark coat covered with a smattering of flakes, kneeled at the side of the grave.

He tried to say a prayer but few words came, for his mind was numb, but he managed to ask for God's blessing on Elizabeth and repeated the Lord's prayer. Then he took from his pocket the love spoon he had made, and with his bare hands scooped away some of the snow and earth to form a shallow trench. He laid the spoon in the trench, replaced the soil and covered the brown scar with loose snow. Elizabeth would understand the gift better than garbled words. He stood up and looked at the headstone.

Already the sculptured words, hastily but meticulously inscribed by the local mason, were barely visible beneath a coating of snow, so he reached out and rubbed it away. Gradually the lettering came into view.

Here lyeth
Elizabeth Kirkhouse
Beloved wife of Thomas Kirkhouse
Died 3 January 1776
Aged 29

He stared at the name Elizabeth, then suddenly he could see old Janet, speaking to him in his workshop. Her words came to him, as clearly as though she was standing beside him:

"Remember that song, Thomas. Elizabeth was adamant about it. Sing it as often as you can and wherever you can, and then she'll be happy wherever she is. Those were her very last words, so see that you obey them. If you don't everything between you will have been in vain, won't it?"

He nodded as though in reply.

"It wasn't in vain, Elizabeth. Nothing was in vain. I promise you that."

* * * * *

The mabsant celebrating the birth of St. James was held every February in Kenfig Town Hall. Already the main room was crowded with dancers and on the dais Eifion Philips, accompanied by a flautist, was playing furiously. Also on the dais was Thomas Evans, smiling gravely at the couples as they gyrated around the small floor. Eventually the dancing stopped and Eifion stepped forward, mopping his brow.

"That's enough of that for the time being, ladies and gentlemen. Settle yourselves down for the moment you've all been waiting for. Thomas Evans will sing the last of his songs for you—the special one he's composed himself. If it's as good as the rest of his music you're in for a treat."

There was an outburst of applause, quickly terminated as the dancers rushed for seats and good vantage points. Thomas picked up the harp and took a deep, steadying breath.

"It is a special song, ladies and gentlemen, as Eifion has said, composed in honour of a lady I once knew. Those of you who know me will understand why I wrote it. As there are some English guests here tonight I will sing it partly in Welsh and partly in English. It's called 'Y Ferch o'r Scer'—'The Maid of Sker'."

He strummed the opening bar but did not start immediately for a sudden bout of nervousness had seized him. It was the first time he had kept his promise to Elizabeth and, although he had no doubt that the song would be well received by Welsh people, he was unsure of the sophisticated English party which had come all the way from Tŷ Talbot to hear him sing. They seemed very superior and intimidating in their fine London clothes. But he gathered up his courage and began.

Pwylla'r bachgen gwyllt ei anian
'R wyf dan ofnau'n rhwymo'm llaw,
Gwaith cael digon o rybuddion
Wrth gariadon yma a thraw,
'R wy'n rhy ifanc eto i ddianc,
Cym'raf bwyll cyn mynd rhy bell;
Pan bwy'n barod, ryw ddiwarnod
Clwyed gai, os bydd i gwell.

At the end of the verse he glanced quickly around. He need not have worried. Everyone, including the English who could not have understood the words, was staring at him with rapt attention, delight mingled with sadness in every expression; and he knew that the long hours perfecting the air had not been in vain. Encouraged, he changed to English.

Hourly I sigh and hourly languish
For the loveliest on the plain;
Feel warm passion's keenist anguish,
Bound in Cupid's powerful chain.
'Tis best revealing,
Not concealing,
Long those pains with which I strove;
Thy vows plight me,
I'll requite thee
With respect and purest love.

But as he came to the last few words his voice faltered and the sound of the harp became discordant. He stood for a moment in silence, then shook his head as though in desperation. Everyone stared at him, expecting another stanza, but he lowered the harp to the floor. Those nearest him saw that there were tears in his eyes. He opened his mouth to say something, but no words came. Then a few of his friends, who understood, began to clap, and others took up the applause until the hall was resounding with noise. Thomas smiled, grateful for the kindness and certain now that the song would delight the hearts of all who heard it; even, possibly, the hearts of future generations.

But he no longer saw his audience. He was standing on the moorland of Sker. Towards him Elizabeth was running, her hair streaming out behind her. He could even feel the impact of her body as she flung herself into his arms, and the warm texture of her lips as she kissed him. Then they were walking hand in hand along the sea shore to Pwll Dafan, there to lie down on the sand.

He knew then that he would never be able to sing the song without pain—the aching, bitter-sweet pain of his love for the Maid of Sker. That would be with him to the end of his days.

CADENZA

THOMAS EVANS CARRIED out all Elizabeth's wishes. He sang Y Ferch o'r Scer at every mabsant and noson lawen he went to, making it one of the best-loved songs in Wales—a better and longer-lasting memorial than any gravestone. Although he pined for the Maid for the rest of his life, and went away to England for a while, he married in his fiftieth year and had several children. While playing at a ball at Nottage Court he collapsed on hearing of the sudden death of his patron, and died himself a few days later on 30th October, 1819. He was aged ninety-one and was buried in Newton churchyard, near Porthcawl.

ACKNOWLEDGEMENTS

I would like to thank the following for the help they have given me.

The Rev. Ryland Oliver, Vicar of Llangyfelach, for giving me information about the church, its records and the remaining tower; The Rev. Brian Jones, Vicar of Llansamlet, for allowing me to study church records and showing me the painting of the original church; the staff of Glamorgan Record Office, and in particular Miss Hilary Thomas and Mr. Christopher Whitak, for giving me much valuable advice; Mrs. Catherine Williams, of Maesteg, a descendant of Thomas and Elizabeth Kirkhouse, who provided me with information about the Kirkhouse family; Mr. and Mrs. Peter Ayres and the customers of *The Plough and Harrow*, Llansamlet, for trying to find the Maid's tombstone; Mrs. Yolande Owen, for disentangling and typing my scripts; and especially Mr. Alexander Cordell, for having helped and encouraged me from the beginning.